MW01593532

Merrick's Maiden:
Cosmos' Gateway Book 5

By S.E. Smith

Acknowledgments
I would like to thank my husband Steve for believing
in me and being proud enough of me to give me the
courage to follow my dream. I would also like to give
a special thank you to my sister and best friend Linda,
who not only encouraged me to write but who also
read the manuscript. Also to my other friends who
believe in me: Julie, Jackie, Lisa, Sally, Elizabeth
(Beth) and Narelle. The girls that keep me going!
—S.E. Smith

A Very Special Note: This story is for my dad who
came down with Spinal Meningitis when he was 12
and woke up to a silent world. He was the best dad a
girl could ever have and I miss him very, very much.
Thank you, Dad, for being the best father a girl could
wish for and for giving me so many wonderful
memories. I love you~ Susan

Montana Publishing
Science Fiction Romance
MERRICK'S MAIDEN: COSMOS' GATEWAY BOOK 5

Summary: Addie Banks' world has been one of silence since a devastating illness when she was sixteen, but now she's hearing a voice in her head that belongs to a man who isn't human, a man that needs her help.

ISBN: 978-1-942562-47-4 (paperback)
ISBN: 978-1-942562-11-5 (eBook)

Published in the United States by Montana Publishing.

{1. Science Fiction Romance – Fiction. 2. Science Fiction – Fiction. 3. Romance – Fiction.}

www.montanapublishinghouse.com

Synopsis

Merrick Ta'Duran is the powerful leader of the Eastern Mountain Clan on the Prime world of Baade. His people, known as the Ghosts of the Forests, live high in the Eastern mountains. Merrick feels the weight of responsibility as the males within his clan become desperate to find mates among the few remaining females. When word comes that a new species has been discovered, he knows he must do what is right for his people - even if it means traveling to a strange, alien realm to do it.

Merrick's world changes when he is injured and captured by a ruthless group of humans. Drugged and held against his will, he is the subject of experiments and testing as the humans try to discover where he came from and duplicate his strength and ability to heal quickly. After months of captivity, he fears his life will end on the strange world until one chance encounter gives him hope.

Addie Banks' world has been one of silence since a devastating illness when she was sixteen. Determined to stand on her own two feet, she goes to school during the day and works at night to put herself through college. Her life unexpectedly changes when she stumbles across something she wasn't supposed to see while at work. Now, she hears a voice in her head - and it is driving her crazy. Her only hope for peace is to help the creature talking to her escape from the men holding him.

Merrick knows the female who helps him is his bond mate. She may deny it. She may fight it. She may even try to run from it, but it won't matter. She is his and he will do everything he can to convince her, hold her, even kidnap her if that is what it takes to make her realize that they belong together.

Will Addie hear the love and longing in Merrick's voice? Can she trust and accept the new life he has to offer? Or, will a ruthless killer silence him before she gets a chance?

Contents

Chapter 1
Six years before:

"Hi, Addie! Are you coming to the party this weekend?" Pam asked as she came up behind Addie in the hallway at Centennial High School in Portland, Oregon.

Addie Banks pushed her blonde hair back with a tired sigh. She hadn't been feeling well all day, but didn't want to miss the big chemistry test she had spent two days studying her butt off for. A shiver shook her thin frame as she gave Pam a smile.

"I hope so," Addie said as she closed her backpack and slung it over her shoulder. "I'm not feeling so good. I'm not staying after school today. Ted said he would give me a ride home."

Pam wrinkled her nose. Ted was Addie's best bud, even if he wasn't one of the 'in' guys to hang with. Honestly, she didn't know what Addie saw in the guy except that he had lived next door to her since kindergarten. The guy was such a dork and had a face that looked like it had been put through a meat grinder since he turned thirteen.

"I don't know why you hang out with Ted," Pam muttered, turning and running her eyes appreciatively over a couple of the boys that walked by. "He's such a dweeb. It's just going to hurt your image if you are seen in his car, you know that, don't you?"

Addie would have rolled her eyes at Pam's self-centered attitude if her head hadn't hurt so damn bad. Instead, she turned toward the doors leading out to the parking lot. She was just thankful the day was over and she could go home.

"Ted is a really sweet guy," Addie replied, walking toward the exit. "His face isn't that bad. He has a minor acne problem, but it is clearing up."

"He has braces!" Pam retorted as Ted walked up to them.

"Which means he'll have straight teeth when he gets them off," Addie replied in exasperation.

"Hi Ted," Pam mumbled, giving Ted a false smile.

"Hey, Pam," Ted grinned as he reached for Addie's backpack. "I'll carry that, Addie. It looks heavy."

"Thanks, Ted," Addie breathed easier as she felt the heavy weight disappear. "I'll talk to you later, Pam."

"'K," Pam replied. "Call me later."

"I will," Addie said, wincing and shivering. "Thanks for giving me a ride, Ted."

"Anytime, Addie," Ted replied, looking at Addie's flushed face. "Are you okay?"

"I'm not feeling too good," Addie admitted.

* * *

Addie waved as Ted pulled out of the driveway. She had told him he could just park at his house two houses down, but he had said it was no big deal to drop her off since she wasn't feeling good. She didn't want to tell him that that was an understatement. She was freezing and hurt all over.

Addie pushed open the front door and dropped her backpack on the floor. A low moan escaped her as she touched her head. Her forehead was burning up.

"Mom?" Addie called out, gripping the back of the couch as she stumbled. "Mom?"

"I'm in the kitchen," her mom called back. "You're home early."

"I... Mom, I don't feel so good," Addie choked out as another wave of excruciating pain swept through her head.

"What?" Helen Banks said as she stepped into the living room. "Addie!"

Addie heard her mother's cry, but it sounded as if it was from the end of a long tunnel. The pain in her head exploded and she felt her body falling. Fear and panic swept through her as her muscles suddenly began jerking by themselves. The cry for help was frozen in her throat as wave after wave of pain swamped her body before darkness finally overcame her.

Addie woke several times. She heard her mom's pleas and her dad's quiet questions, but they were disjointed and sounded strange. She was vaguely aware of flashing lights and blurred images of people around her frantically talking. The sunlight sent shafts of pain through her, sending her back into the darkness.

A little while later, she felt her body being lifted again. She tried to focus on what was happening, but the rapidly flashing lights overhead made her nauseous. Afraid, she closed her eyes. A silent tear escaped and slid down the side of her face.

I don't want to die, she thought vaguely. *I have so much to live for.*

* * *

Four days later, Addie blinked sleepily. A frown creased her brow as she looked at a balloon floating by the bed. The words 'Get Well Soon' in a middle of the Teddy Bear's stomach confused her. Her eyes moved to the flowers in the windowsill.

She turned when she felt a movement on her right side. Her mom was standing up and leaning over her. A concerned smile curved Addie's lips as she stared up at her mom. Tears were streaming down her mom's tired face.

Addie tilted her head, puzzled. She saw her mom's mouth moving, but nothing was coming out of it. Her head turned when the door opened. She blinked again when she saw a man in a white coat. Her eyes flickered to the name on it, . W. H. Harris.

"Hi, Addie, I'm Doctor Harris," the man said as he came to stand next to the bed.

"She just woke up," Helen said in relief. "Addie, how are you feeling, honey?"

Addie glanced back and forth as fear, panic, and confusion swept through her. She saw their mouths moving, but she couldn't hear what was being said. Raising her right hand, she weakly touched her ear to see if there was anything covering them. Her fingers skimmed over her ear.

"Addie, what is it?" Helen asked, threading her fingers through Addie's when she held her hand out to her.

"I can't hear you," Addie whispered, staring up at her mom. "Mom, why can't I hear you?"

Helen Banks' eyes widened in horror. Addie's eyes jerked from her mother to the doctor as they stared down at her in concern. She saw him move his lips, but she didn't know what he was saying. Tears of frustration filled her eyes as she stared back and forth. Why couldn't she hear them?

* * *

Two months later, Addie sat in the back seat of her parent's Honda CRV staring blindly out the window. She knew her parents were talking, but she didn't bother trying to figure out what they were saying. They had just left another specialist, the fifth in as many weeks.

No tears burned her eyes this time. She had promised herself that she wouldn't cry any more. She was tired of crying, it didn't do any good. Since the day she woke up in the hospital, there had been too many. She had cried, ranted, and finally just pulled away from everyone.

At first, the silence almost suffocated her. She was used to always having some type of background noise on. She loved listening to music and talking with her parents and friends. Shoot, she even talked to herself when there was no one else to talk to!

Now, there was nothing. She was beginning to understand some of the things being said between the doctors and her parents by watching their expressions and picking out a few words on their lips.

This specialist told them the same thing as the others. It was very likely that she would never be able to hear again. The high, prolonged fever from the bacterial Spinal Meningitis she had contracted had silenced her world forever. They believed she contracted it from swimming at their cottage house the weekend before.

Addie watched dispassionately as a motorcycle stopped next to them. She couldn't hear the rumble of it as the guy waited for the light to turn green. She placed her hand against the glass, feeling the vibration from it, instead. Closing her eyes, a deep sadness washed over her. Never again would she hear the sounds that she had taken for granted. A silent tear ran down her cheek. She let it.

Maybe there was room for one more tear, she thought as it finally sank in that she would never hear again. *Just one more.*

Chapter 2
Present Day:

Merrick Ta'Duran gritted his teeth against the pain as he felt another blow to his back. He refused to release his grip on the male's throat he held in his hands. His body suddenly jerked as a powerful bolt of electricity ran through it. Two probes, attached to long strands of wire, dug into his skin. With a last twist, he heard the satisfying sound of bone breaking.

"Shit! That's the third guard he's killed," a voice yelled. "Hit him again!"

Merrick released the body, collapsing down onto the floor on one knee as another surge of electricity hit him. He fought against the debilitating assault, but one after another struck him. It took five this time to bring him down. He was building a tolerance to it. It was either that, or the rage and desire to finally be free of the constant pain was driving his resistance up.

"Chain him," the voice of the male said in disgust. "And get rid of the body."

"Are you just going to let him get away with killing Ray?" Another voice asked in astonishment.

"Ray killed himself when he disobeyed a direct order not to enter the cell," Weston Wright retorted in disgust. "We need him alive. Now, do what I ordered or I'll lock your ass in here with him."

"Fuck that," the man grumbled as he pulled the chains toward Merrick as several men stood holding him down with long rods filled with an explosive charge. "I don't fucking get paid enough for this."

"You can always be replaced, Mr. Crawford," Wright replied. "Everyone in here can be replaced except the creature you're chaining, remember that."

Bradley Crawford grunted a response. He knew what the word 'replace' meant. It meant dead, just like it had for Ray and the other two men.

Brad snapped the locks back around the wrists of the huge male lying on the floor. A shiver ran through him when the man's eerie silver eyes turned to look at him. He swore it looked as if there were tiny flames in the center of them.

"He's secured again," Bradley said, tripping over Ray's body as he tried to get away from Merrick.

"Get rid of the body," Wright said turning away. "And hire another guard."

"Damn it," Bradley grumbled as he pulled Ray's body out of the cell by the arms. "I fucking hate this job."

* * *

Merrick watched dispassionately from where he lay on the hard, cold floor as the door to his cell was closed again. He had been moved to a new one late yesterday. This one had thick bars all the way around it, allowing them to see him visually without the use of their cameras. The only thing in it was a long, narrow bed bolted to the floor, a toilet, and a sink.

He had been moved from the one with solid walls after he broke loose from the chains holding him and destroyed the cameras in the old cell that were monitoring him. When the guards came in, he had been ready. He had killed two of them before the others rushed him with their stun guns and sedatives.

He had managed to kill this male when he came in alone. The male's taunts had died on his lips as Merrick wrapped one of the chains used to hold him around the human's neck. A nasty smile curved Merrick's lips as he thought of the dead human.

"I'm going to beat the shit out of you," Ray had promised as he tapped the metal rod in his hand. "You killed Bill. I liked Bill. I can't kill your ass, but I can make sure you wish you were dead."

Merrick had already wished that a hundred times over the past four months. He lowered his face to the cold floor and rested his cheek against it. His muscles were contracting and releasing in reaction to the powerful charges he had been struck with. Even his heart stuttered for a moment as it tried to find the correct rhythm again.

"Goddess, help me," he whispered as he closed his eyes. "Give me the peace of death if you will not give me a way to release myself."

It was not like him to wish for death, but the continued testing was slowly draining his resolve. His body and mind had been tested over and over. There were two men and one woman he would kill if given a chance.

Never in his life had he thought he would want to harm a female, but the old human was one he would not think twice about eliminating from this world if he got the chance. Teriff 'Tag Krell Manok, leader of the Prime, might have thought that the human males were untrustworthy, but they were nothing compared to the female. The tests she ordered were far worse than the beatings he received from the males.

He had all but given up hope that he would be found. No... if he was to survive, it would be by his own resources. Pushing away his earlier weakness, Merrick twisted and pushed himself up on trembling arms. He forced himself up into a sitting position in an effort to push back the fatigue crushing him.

Wincing as he slid along the slick, concrete floor, he rested his back against the narrow bed frame. His eyes swept his new location. This one was different from the others. The room wasn't very large. The cage he was in took up almost a fourth of it.

There was a long, stainless steel table against the far wall and a row of cabinets on the far side with a sink. It looked like another exam room. This time, it might be his last one.

The humans holding him never stayed in one place for more than a few weeks. He had lost count over the past months how many times he had been drugged and awakened in a new holding cell.

Merrick closed his eyes and thought back to the night he had been captured. It had only been his promise to his clan, that he would find women capable of being bond mates, that had brought him to this world. Now... now, not only had he failed to help his people, he had endangered them by being taken.

He had been helping the human male, Cosmos Raines, try to protect Tansy Bell and two other Earth women. Tansy was an agent for her government. Personally, Merrick thought that Mak 'Tag Krell Manok, the huge middle son of Teriff, should have just tossed the small female over his shoulder and returned to their world with her. The same thing should have been done to the other two women involved, as well. It was too dangerous to let the women who were bond mates to a Prime warrior be involved in such dangerous work.

Instead, Mak had allowed the female to continue on her dangerous assignment. His mind drifted, replaying the night once again as if it were just happening. He knew that Tansy was trying to protect her own leader, President Askew Thomas, from being assassinated by his Vice-President. Unfortunately, something had gone wrong during the mission.

* * *

Four months earlier:

"You shouldn't allow the females of your world to take such risks," Merrick muttered as he stared at all the equipment glowing in the van. "Mak should have tied Tansy up and taken her back to our world."

Cosmos glanced over his shoulder with a raised eyebrow. "You saw Tansy. Do you really think she would have just stood by while Mak tried to tie her up? Hell, he would have been the one needing help. Tansy, Helene, and Natasha are not the kind of women you tie up unless they let you," Cosmos replied with a twisted grin. "Shit, any one of them could take my ass out in a heartbeat before I even knew it and I'm no slouch when it comes to hand-to-hand combat."

Merrick scowled. "Why do the women of your world take such risks? Why do the males allow it?" He demanded, folding his arms across his chest as he leaned against the inside wall of the van.

"Dude, didn't you just hear what I said?" Cosmos asked in exasperation. "It's not like this in every country, though we are working on it, but women have a right to make their own decisions and choices about their lives. Tansy, Natasha, and Helene chose to protect those that can't protect themselves. They fight beside men and women around the world who are trying to make this a better place to live. Hell, I'm just glad we have the Tansy's of the world. We sure the hell need more like her."

Merrick frowned as he listened to Cosmos explain that Tansy's work had brought down some of the major drug and slavery rings around the world. Helene, and her sister, Natasha, did the same type of work in Russia. Without them, many of the Organized Crime Gangs would have been impossible to infiltrate.

"If I found my bond mate, I would keep her safe," Merrick muttered under his breath as he watched one of Cosmos' men adjust a camera showing Tansy talking to a male. "I would never allow her to do something that was so dangerous."

Cosmos glanced over his shoulder again and shook his head. "Why don't you stretch your legs outside for a few minutes? You can scan the area for us as well to make sure it is clear. Just looking at you folded up in here is making my legs hurt."

"Good idea," Merrick grunted with a relieved nod as he reached for the handle of the door before he paused to look back at Cosmos. "I don't know why you don't just kill the men you are after. You know that they are trying to harm your leader. Wouldn't that make more sense than endangering the women?"

"Yeah, it makes more sense. Unfortunately, our laws are a little different than yours," Cosmos replied, before he turned back to look at Tansy smiling seductively at her target. "Not that Tansy gives a rat's ass about that if she is given half a chance to take out the bad guys."

"You live in a strange world, human," Merrick muttered, shaking his head as he opened the back door of the van and stepped out.

He had barely closed it when two black vehicles suddenly appeared at the far end of the narrow alley. Men poured from the vehicles and began moving toward the van. He knew immediately that something had gone wrong.

"Cosmos!" Merrick growled in a low voice, jerking the door open again. "Men are coming down the alley."

"Shit! We've been compromised! All units, take cover, we have been compromised," Cosmos warned into the headset he was wearing before he jerked it off his head and nodded to the other three men in the van with them. "Keep Tansy, Helene, and Natasha in your sight," he instructed one of the men. "How many?"

Merrick glanced around the side of the van. "Ten," he replied. "I'll take out the ones on the right. Can I kill them?"

"Leave one alive, if you can," Cosmos responded, checking his gun as he climbed out of the van. "We need to know how they knew we were here."

"I will try," Merrick said before giving Cosmos a short nod of warning. "Now," he muttered, turning and running toward the five men on the right side of the alley.

Gunfire had lit the night. He had taken three bullets, one in the arm, one to his upper thigh, and one had grazed his left side. While they hurt, none of them had been life threatening.

He cursed the primitive weapons Cosmos insisted that he carry. They were clumsy and unfamiliar in his hands. He had finally abandoned them. Chasing the lone man down the alley, he had rounded the corner only to find he had run into a trap.

He had fought, leaving more dead than alive as another group of men surrounded him. His eyes flickered open as he remembered the image of one man who stepped out of the darkness as he collapsed. The man had been shorter than him, but was thickly built. He carried a long gun that shot darts, instead of the pieces of metal the others used.

The darts contained an agent in them that paralyzed his muscles. The man, Markham, was the first man he wanted to kill. The ugly, but satisfied, smile on the male's face burned through his mind.

"I heard the reports of an unusual man in Russia who had helped my target escape," Markham had commented as he knelt beside him on the hard ground. "My employer wanted to know who could kill like that. It would appear the elusive Ms. Bell has more than her family and Cosmos Raines up her sleeve. I think my employer will be very interested in keeping you alive… for a short time, at least."

* * *

Merrick remembered reaching out in a fit of rage to kill the man. The last thing he remembered of that night was Markham striking him with the butt of the gun in his hands. Since then, he had seen the man on three other occasions. Markham's gloating gaze built his resolve to kill the man before he returned to his world or die trying.

He leaned his head back and stared up at the ceiling as exhaustion pulled at him, making him want to give into the need for sleep. Another shudder wracked his body as the after effects of the shocks he had been hit with ran through him. He desperately needed to escape.

His thoughts turned to his home world of Baade. Sadness coursed through him at the devastation that had been wrought by the declining birth rate of Prime females. Most of the eligible women on Baade were spoken for as soon as they came of age.

He and the other males were matched to their mates through a mating rite's ceremony held twice a year. The ceremony was a gathering of all the unmatched males and females. They were presented to each other in small groups, rotating until the markings appeared, proving they were destined to be together. If in cases such as his, no match was made, the warrior was left with one of two choices; continue to attend the ceremonies in the hope he would find his bond mate or resign himself to a solitary existence.

The chemical change that occurred when a Prime male came in contact with a female genetically ideal to them, could not be fraudulently recreated. The powerful chemical caused a physical and emotional reaction in the male, that bonded him to a female. The males become overwhelmed with feelings of possessiveness, protectiveness, and sexual desire.

In addition a mating mark, a series of intricate circles denoting the unbreakable bond between mates, appeared on the palm of the male and the matching female when they came into contact with each other. Each mark was as individual as the bonded pair. It would not appear until the male and female reached the age of mating.

Procreation was impossible without such a connection. Their scientists discovered the chemical reaction was an evolution of their genetic makeup. As far as he knew, they had not found a solution to the problem. If a resolution wasn't found soon, the Prime species was destined for extinction.

A reluctant smile curved Merrick's lips as he thought of the unusual answer that suddenly appeared before his species in the form of a tiny human female. Jasmine 'Tinker' Bell had unexpectedly appeared on J'Kar 'Tag Krell Manok's warship through a Gateway connecting their two worlds. The Gateway, created by Cosmos Raines, had given his world and the men living on it hope for a future.

Merrick looked at his palms. Nothing showed on them and probably never would. It didn't matter. He had not come to this world for himself, but for the men under his command. As the leader of the Eastern Mountain clan, it was his duty to guide them and do whatever he could to ensure their survival.

He and his cousin, Core, had journeyed to the capital of Prime after they captured a human male. The male had lied to them. It was the first taste of deceit from the humans that Merrick had experienced. His fingers rose to touch his ear as he thought of J'kar's tiny mate. A small chuckle escaped him. She had been the first taste he had of a human female's ferocious ability to protect those that she loved.

Tink had attacked him when he struck out at her mate. She had jumped on his back, covered his eyes, and bitten his ear with her smooth teeth. Her mother had kicked him in his groin while her sister had knocked him out with a planter. He shook his head as the memories flooded him.

No, not all humans are traitorous. Including the males, he reluctantly admitted as he thought of Cosmos and those working with him. *There are those that can be trusted here just as there are on my world, and those that cannot.*

His eyes flickered up as the door opened and Weston and three other men stepped into the room. Weston eyed him with a combination of consternation and hatred. Merrick returned the human's stare.

"Knock him out," Weston ordered. "Doctor Rockman wants another sample."

Merrick surged up to his feet at the name of the female doctor. The roar he emitted loudly echoed in the room as Weston raised the syringe in his hand. It took three men pulling on the chains to get him close enough to the bars for Weston to inject him. It would have been impossible if he wasn't still weak from his earlier fight.

Merrick slid down his hands and knees on the floor as the drug rushed through him. His arms trembled violently as he fought against it, but it was impossible. He slowly collapsed down to the cold floor again. For a moment, his heart stuttered and paused as the excessive amount of the drug they used flowed through his bloodstream.

Perhaps this will be the last time, he thought as darkness descended around him.

Chapter 3

Addie waved her badge at Ted and smiled. He smiled and waved back before pressing the button to lift the security gate. She lifted her foot off the brake and let her small dark blue Kia Sonata roll over the speed bump before depressing the accelerator. Turning right into the parking lot, she headed for the employee entrance.

She grimaced as she glanced at the clock on the dash. She was running a few minutes late. A silent chuckle escaped her and she rolled her eyes.

Who would give a rat's ass that I'm not there to mop the floor or empty a trash can on time? She thought with a grin at the deserted parking lot.

It was almost ten o'clock on a Friday night. Everyone who worked at Keiser Research was gone for the weekend except the poor suckers like her, Ted and a few other security guards. A sigh escaped Addie as she pulled into a parking space up close to the back entrance and turned the engine off.

Grabbing her thick, long blonde hair in one hand, she wound a hair band around it and pulled it into a ponytail to keep it out of her way. She glanced around to make sure she had her badge to get in the building. She had only been working there a few days.

Opening the driver's door, she checked that she had her car keys and small, leather wallet before locking it. Her eyes ran over the outside of the building. She hadn't worked in this section yet. The email she received today instructed her to come to this building instead of the main office complex on the south side of the parking lot.

Swiping her badge in the security lock, she waited as the light turned green before she pulled the door open. At least this one had a light! The main complex didn't and since she couldn't hear the sound of the lock disengaging, she had to try to time when it would unlock. If she tried too soon, it didn't work. If she tried too late, it didn't work.

Addie sighed as the door closed behind her. She reached into her back pocket and pulled out the map of the building. She would need to check in with the guard in the front lobby first. Ted was supposed to have talked to the guy for her and explained that she was deaf.

Walking down the main corridor, she thought of Ted and Pam. It was hard to believe that Miss High and Mighty, 'he-is-going-to-ruin-your-reputation Pam', had fallen in love with Ted during the last half of their senior year! Ted was one of the few kids that had remained in contact with her after she moved to St. Augustine to attend the Florida School for the Deaf and Blind. After she graduated, she moved back to Portland and began taking classes while working a wide variety of jobs.

When she had casually 'mentioned' a couple of weeks ago that she needed to get a second job to help cover the cost of her last class, he had helped her get the position on the housekeeping staff at Keiser where he worked nights as the gate security guard. Addie was trying everything she could to remain independent from her parents.

It had taken her the last two years to earn enough to move out into her own place while she attended college. A shudder went through her as she thought of her mom's insistence that she remain at home where they could take care of her. While her parents had been the driving force of her going to St. Augustine to finish her schooling, they had been adamant about her returning home as soon as she graduated.

It had taken the combined forces of her five older siblings to get her parents to agree to her attending college. She had agreed to live at home for the first two years. What she hadn't told her parents was that she had spent a lot of that time working several part-time jobs to save up enough money to move out. She loved her parents to death, but their over-protectiveness, especially her mom's need to know everything she was doing, was driving her crazy!

No, if it meant mopping floors to help supplement my income while I finish the last class I am taking to get my certification as a licensed massage therapist, then, I'll mop a hundred of them, she thought as she stepped up to the guard station.

Addie had one more test the following afternoon before she finished her degree. Once she got her license, she could quit working here and work as a Masseuse while she continued to work on her Master's degree in Physical Therapy. Each step was leading to her dream of opening her own clinic one day. With a degree in both Massage and Physical Therapy, she knew she could make it without ever having to depend on anyone else ever again!

Addie drew in a deep breath and gave a brief, polite smile to the guard sitting in the chair with his feet propped up on the desk. A shiver of distaste washed through her when he ran his gaze over her. Ignoring the appreciative look in his eyes, she waited for the guard closest to her to respond to her presence. He seemed to have difficulty pulling his eyes from one of the monitors. Holding up her badge, she handed it to him so he could scan it when he finally looked at her.

"She's a hot one," the guard sitting behind the one scanning her badge said with a smooth smile. "Maybe she would be interested in a little nighttime organization of the supply closet."

"Shut up, Josh," Bradley muttered.

"Why? Ted said she's deaf. She can't hear what the fuck I'm saying," Josh chuckled. "You can't hear me saying I want to bend you over and fuck that sweet ass of yours, can you, sweetheart?"

Addie composed her face to have that 'I'm blonde and clueless' look on it. She had met too many assholes over the years to let him get to her. The one good thing about being deaf was that she had learned really quick who to avoid. One of the first things she had learned was to read lips and expressions.

Being aware of what was going on had actually saved her life on two previous occasions. Both times, she had read the intention of the guys. The first time had been when she had gone to the beach on a date during high school. The guy had slipped a drug into her can of soda. She would have drank it if he hadn't bragged about it to his friend as he was handing it to her.

The second time was as she was leaving the bar shortly after her twenty-first birthday. There had been a guy in the bar watching her all night long. It wasn't so much what he said, but the way he was looking at her that sent a shaft of warning through her. She had made sure that she was never alone. Three days later, she saw the guy on the news. He had attacked another girl after following her from the same nightclub.

"Just shut up," Bradley muttered in annoyance. "Clean these areas."

Addie looked down at the map the guard had printed out for her. He circled several sections and wrote the word 'Clean thoroughly' up at the top of the paper before handing it to her. Addie nodded her head and took the map.

"Hey, don't go down to the third level," Bradley called out to her as the phone rang.

"Asshole, she can't hear you," Josh chuckled as he watched Addie's ass as she walked down the hallway. "Damn, I wouldn't mind having a piece of that."

* * *

Merrick jerked awake and rolled. He barely made it to the toilet before the contents of his stomach emptied. He didn't know what they had pumped into him this time, but he could feel his body rejecting it. Heaving, he gripped the bars until the nausea passed.

Several minutes later, he slowly straightened. With a softly muttered curse, he released the bars and stepped over to the sink. He twisted the knob for the cold water. Bending, he washed his mouth out before washing his face. It took several minutes before he felt slightly better.

Standing back straight, he rolled his shoulders. The chains around his wrists rattled as he pushed his hair back from his face. The faint memories of hands on his body sent a ripple of distaste and rage through him. His stomach churned again, but this time for a different reason. He turned back to the bed and stripped the thin cover off of the mattress. Tearing a strip from it, he dampened it and quickly wiped his body down to get rid of the feel of Dr. Rockman's hands on it.

He closed his eyes as his hands slipped under the waistband of the thin, cotton pants he wore. He cleaned himself as thoroughly as he could before tossing the cloth against the bars in fury. Throwing his head back, he bit back the loud roar that threatened to escape him. He would not give the guards the satisfaction of knowing how violated he felt.

His eyes moved to the door when he heard the sound of footsteps outside it. The lights were off in the room, but the darkness did not bother his vision. Moving to the side of the cage so the thick corner sections of it partially concealed him, he waited as the sound of the lock disengaging echoed in the cold room. Perhaps he would get the chance to kill another one of the guards.

A cold smile curved his lips as the door opened and the light came on. His eyes narrowed when the door opened wider and he saw a slender figure backing into it. Long blonde hair, piled into a messy ponytail, hung down the back of what had to be a female. He couldn't see her face, yet. She appeared to be trying to pull a large cart into the room.

Amusement and curiosity reluctantly tugged at his lips when a low, muttered curse escaped her when the cart became stuck in the opening. He watched as the figured straightened and groaned as her gloved hands moved to her lower back. She rubbed it as if she was in pain.

A tired sigh escaped her this time and she leaned forward to grab something off the cart. He stiffened until he realized that she had turned to the counter. His eyes followed her as she sprayed foam on the countertop before wiping it down. She did the same to the cabinets and sink.

A soft growl escaped him when she bent over and opened the trash can to pull the bag out. The movement pulled the black cloth trousers she was wearing tight over her ass. Merrick frowned in annoyance. First, because he didn't understand why his body was reacting to the female with such an unexpected intensity. The second reason was because he knew she must have heard the sound that escaped him, but she continued to clean the room as if he wasn't there.

He watched as she pulled a long stick out of a yellow bucket. She pressed the strings until most of the water was removed before she started cleaning the floor. A frown creased his brow when he noticed she still hadn't turned around to look at the cage. The need to see what her face looked like was beginning to grow to an irritating, but persistent ache.

The frown darkened as she tiredly brushed her cheek against her shoulder. It was obvious from her demeanor that she either had no idea he was there, or she was pretending. He rattled the chain on his arm against the metal bar to draw her attention. His brow furrowed suspiciously when she still didn't turn around.

It must be another test, he thought as the murderous rage he had felt earlier swept through him.

Dr. Rockman had tried to 'research' his mating habits once before. She had a drugged-up woman brought in two months ago at the previous place they kept him. The foul smelling female had taken one look at him, licked her lips, and run her eyes over him as if she had been given something sweet to eat.

The look of desire on her face hadn't lasted long once he proved he wasn't interested. Her screams and wretched cries for help had echoed once she came close enough for him to wrap his hands around her neck. He would never mate with such a female, no matter how desperate he might become.

He continued to follow the movements of the woman as she ran the mop from side to side. He tugged on the chains holding him. Frustration burned through him when he realized that he couldn't reach through the bars far enough to grab her. She would have to actually be against them before he would be able to touch her.

All thoughts flew from his mind when she suddenly turned until she was facing him. A soft squeak escaped her and her eyes widened in shock when she saw that she wasn't alone. Dark green eyes stared back at him in surprise before it was replaced with confusion as she noted the bars and the shackles around his wrists.

A low, menacing snarl escaped him when her eyes returned to his. His own glittering gaze captured and held hers for several long seconds as they both assessed the other. It took him half that time to realize that the feeling of rage had been replaced with another emotion. An emotion that he wasn't quite sure how to describe.

He impatiently waited for her to speak. The frown marring his brow deepened when the silence dragged on as they continued to stare at each other. He finally released a frustrated grunt when she blinked in slow motion, as if she wasn't sure if he was real or not.

Merrick watched the female's face as a multitude of emotions swept over it. Surprise, confusion, uncertainty, and finally, curiosity glittered in the expressive green depths. Another jolt of unease ran through him as he felt himself being pulled into their brilliant depths. He tightly clenched the bars in aggravation knowing that he would never be able to reach the woman from this distance. His lip curled in warning as a figure suddenly appeared in the hallway behind her.

"Hey! What are you doing in here?" A voice demanded angrily behind her.

Merrick's eyes flickered from her to the guard called Crawford before moving back to her. He watched as she turned to look at the man in confusion. Her eyes flickered back and forth between him and the guard. A low growl of warning escaped him when Crawford pulled the cart out of the doorway and caught the door before it could close.

The female stumbled backwards away from the guard when he pushed the door hard enough that it banged against the wall. Her foot caught in the tangled strands of the mop and she lost her balance, falling against the bars of his cage.

Triumph filled him as he wound his fingers into her hair, pulling her close enough for him to wrap the fingers of his other hand around her neck. The triumph quickly changed to surprise when an electrical shock flashed through his fingers the moment he touched her skin. It was so unexpected that he jerked back, releasing her.

"Damn it," Crawford snapped, reaching out and grabbing the female by her forearm and jerking her away from the bars. "Get the fuck out of here!"

Merrick slammed into the bars at the woman's cry of pain when the guard roughly pulled her away. He hit his fists against the bars again and flashed his teeth, which had elongated, at the guard when he continued to push her toward the door. An overwhelming need to capture and protect the female swept through him.

"Holy shit!" Crawford whispered, stumbling backwards after the woman who was staring at Merrick with a combination of horror, confusion, and fear. "They didn't say nothing about you being a Vampire."

Merrick's eyes glowed with silver flames and he knew his face was distorted into a mask of rage as he stared at the woman who was holding her left hand protectively against her chest. Her eyes widened even more when she saw his eyes glowing with a fierce possessiveness at her before the contact between them was broken. Crawford jerked open the door and pushed the female through it before pulling it closed behind him.

Merrick struck the metal bars again. Stepping back, he stared at the door in disbelief and confusion. His eyes slowly lowered to his clenched fist while his mind swirled with a barrage of unexpected thoughts. Uncurling his fingers, he stared down at the delicate pattern forming in the center of his palm. The intricate patterns seemed to mock his earlier thoughts.

I have to escape, he thought with a growing determination as he clenched his fist and raised it to his chest. His eyes moved to the door. *I have a mate.*

Chapter 4

Addie stared at the guard with a combination of fear and confusion. She absently rubbed at her arm where he had grabbed her. She knew she would have bruises from his fingers.

She didn't understand what had just happened or why there was a guy locked up in the exam room she was cleaning. Her eyes flickered to the door, then back to the guard. She stumbled backwards when he turned furiously on her and shook his head.

"You don't go in there!" He ordered, pointing to the door in aggravation before he looked back at her. "You didn't see anything, do you understand? Nothing! They will kill you if they knew you saw him."

Addie's eyes widened when he pointed his fingers at his eyes and shook his head vehemently at her. She slowly nodded her head. Raising a trembling finger to the corner of her eye, then down to her lips, she slowly shook her head.

* * *

Crawford released the breath he had been holding. He had caught a glimpse of the cart in the hallway video monitor and rushed downstairs. Fortunately, Josh had changed places with Ted for a scheduled break. Josh would have reported the incident immediately and shit would've hit the fan, or worse.

I would've been dealing with another dead body, he thought in growing aggravation.

Ted didn't know what was going on. He just nodded when Bradley told him to stay put at the upstairs desk until he got back. Now, Bradley turned back to glare at the frightened green eyes staring at him. In the back of his mind, he knew he should report what he had seen, but he wouldn't. Reporting that the new girl assigned to housekeeping had seen whatever in the hell the creature was in the other room would've opened a shitload of other questions.

This wasn't what he had signed on for when he accepted the fucking job as a security guard. Drawing in a deep breath, he released it. Pulling a pen and a piece of paper out of his front shirt pocket, he quickly scribbled down a note for Addie.

He waited as she tentatively reached for it. Her eyes stayed locked with his for several long seconds before she dropped it to the paper in her hand. She frowned and bit her lip as she read the brief line.

Say nothing and you won't get hurt. Understand?!

He nodded his head at the cart when she raised her head and looked at him again. A frown darkened his features when she jerked back against the wall as he reached out and snatched the paper out of her hand. He crumpled it up, scowling in frustration when she slid along the wall before hurrying to push the cart back down toward the elevators.

"I fucking *hate* this job," he muttered as he followed her.

* * *

Addie breathed a sigh of relief as she pushed the door to the building open and exited it. She glanced over her shoulder where the guard from earlier stood watching her. He had followed her as she returned the cleaning cart to the janitorial closet before escorting her to the exit.

Focusing on her car, she hurried over to where it was parked. Her fingers were trembling so badly it took her three tries before she could press the unlock button on the remote. It was only when she was safely locked inside that she stopped to think about what she had seen.

It had been almost two-thirty in the morning when she went into the exam room. That had been the last level of the night that she needed to clean before she could go home. She had been so tired that she was running on autopilot. It had taken everything in her to just lift the mop. Since every other room had been empty, she had assumed that one would be as well.

Sighing again, she shook her head and started the engine. She didn't understand what was going on. After the first moment of surprise, she had thought it was someone participating in a test group. She had just finished a class where several of the students had signed up to be in one study group or another to earn extra money. It might have made sense if Crawford hadn't written that note. *Say nothing and you won't get hurt.*

Why would anyone want to hurt her for what she had seen? The guy had been chained, as well as, caged. Why? Had she just imagined that his teeth had grown longer, like a Vampire? What was going on with his eyes, too? They had been a strange color and glowed?

This is not what I need right now in my life, Addie groaned to herself even as she waved her hand to Ted as he raised the gate for her. *I just want to finish my degrees and open my own business.*

Addie glanced back and forth before turning onto the deserted street. Biting her lip, she couldn't help remembering the furious expression in the man's eyes as he stared back at her. A shiver escaped her when she remembered the shock she had felt when he first touched her. Rubbing the palm of her left hand on the steering wheel cover, another shiver wracked her body at how sensitive it felt.

I hope life doesn't get any crazier than this, she thought as she turned onto the freeway.

* * *

Forty minutes later, Addie pushed opened the door to her small, one bedroom apartment and tossed her car keys onto the narrow entrance table. Turning, she quickly locked the four deadbolts. Whoever had lived here before had been extremely paranoid. It was either that, or they had a lock fetish. Either way, she decided it wouldn't hurt to use them since they were available.

Ted had re-keyed all the locks for her the day she moved in. That was the good thing about having a Locksmith-slash-security guard as your next door neighbor, she decided. Addie kicked off her tennis shoes by the table and walked into the narrow sitting room.

She didn't bother turning on a light. She always left the one over the stove on. Since the apartment was so small, that one light practically lit the entire thing. Opening the refrigerator, she rubbed her left palm along her pant leg as it itched again. She was thirsty, but didn't want the water, orange juice, or milk on the shelf.

With a grunt, she reached into the door and grabbed the wine cooler that Pam had left last weekend. Tonight was a good night to have something with a little kick to it. Shutting the door, she turned and leaned against it while she used her shirt to twist off the metal cap.

The cold glass felt good against her itching palm. Raising it to her lips, she drank almost a quarter of the Strawberry Daiquiri flavored liquor. Lowering the bottle, she leaned her head back and closed her eyes for a moment.

"Why? Why do they have him chained? Who is he?" Addie whispered out loud.

Even though she couldn't hear the words in her ears, knowing that she could still speak helped ward off the feeling of not being whole sometimes. One of her teachers at the School for the Deaf had shown her how to measure the volume by the force of air she expended in her diaphragm.

According to her teachers, the fact that she lost her hearing at sixteen helped with her understanding of speech patterns and enunciations, making it easier for her to speak in a clear voice. The fact that she didn't speak often was because people tended to think she could hear them. Often times, they would turn away from her when they replied and she hated having to ask them to repeat themselves.

Opening her eyes, she pushed herself away from the refrigerator door and walked into the sitting room. She turned, and half fell-half lowered, herself onto the flowered sofa. Her eyes flickered to the street lights outside. The light looked as if it was dancing because of the wind and trees that lined the front of the apartment building. The nice thing about being on the third floor was that she didn't have to close the blinds most of the time.

"Why?" She asked again, switching the wine cooler to her right hand so she could rub her palm against her leg again.

Addie growled in frustration when the itching got worse. Turning her palm up, she glanced down at it in irritation when the slight sensation of burning and itching continued. Her eyes widened in surprise when she noticed something in the middle of it. Setting the wine cooler on the coffee table, she leaned to the side and turned on the table lamp next to the couch.

Holding her palm under the light, she frowned when she saw a circular design in the center of it. Pushing herself up off the couch, she walked back into the kitchen and opened the drawer where she threw everything that she didn't know what to do with. She pushed aside the manuals to the coffee maker, the scissors that she had been looking for the day before, and a variety of other items before she wrapped her fingers around the small magnifying glass in the back of it.

Closing the drawer, she returned to the couch and balanced her palm on the edge of the armrest. Using the magnify glass, she peered at the mark. Her lips parted in amazement when she saw that inside the circle were what looked like symbols of some sort.

"What the…?" She breathed, blinking to make sure she wasn't seeing things.

Frowning, she stood up again. This time, she headed for the tiny bathroom. Flicking on the light, she walked over to the pedestal sink and turned the water on. Grabbing the bar of soap and her fingernail brush, she began scrubbing at the mark on her hand.

The growl she emitted turned to a startled yelp and the soap and fingernail brush dropped with a rattle to the bottom of the sink when a voice suddenly resounded in her head. A voice that was definitely not hers! Staring up at the mirror in shock, Addie stared at her reflection. Dark green eyes, pale pink lips, a small nose covered with a light dusting of freckles, and a slightly dimpled chin framed by a mass of long, blonde hair gazed back at her.

What… What is a bond mate? She thought back to the voice.

You are my bond mate. It means you belong to me! Tell me your name, the distinctly male voice demanded.

Addie felt a sudden, strange light-headedness cloud her mind. The dizziness threatened to send her to her shaking knees. Gripping the edge of the sink, she sank down onto the toilet, thankful that the lid was down for once. Breathing deeply to keep from fainting, she forced her swirling mind to go blank.

* * *

Merrick leaned back on the bed in his narrow cell. The fatigue and anger that had consumed him for the past months still burned inside him, but so did another emotion. He stared at the palm of his hand with a sense of amazement and wonder. He had found his mate.

His eyes flickered to the door when it opened. The corner of his lip pulled up into a sneer. Crawford glanced at him and blanched. The man was nervous as he stepped into the room.

Merrick kept his eyes on the male as he closed the door. He didn't get up off the bed. Instead, he waited to see what the male wanted. A low oath escaped Crawford and he stunk with fear.

"Listen...," Crawford began before he stopped to clear his throat. "I know... I think... Hell, can you understand me?"

Merrick watched the nervous twitch at the corner of Crawford's right eye. The smell of the man and his body's reaction were not something the human could fake. He debated whether he should respond. This was the first time that this human had approached him alone and he was curious as to what he wanted. Merrick finally inclined his head in acknowledgement of the question.

"What happened tonight...," Crawford paused and drew in a deep breath again. "Listen, you can't tell anyone about the girl coming in here. The docs... I don't know what the others might do to her. It is bad enough as it is. I don't want to be responsible for any more deaths. Hell, I just want to get out of this mess in one piece! I didn't know that they... who these people were... I just needed a job after I got out of the Army. My girl is pregnant and I needed to earn some money to support us. Shit, this is all a fucking mess."

Merrick watched as the man cursed under his breath again and ran his hand over the back of his neck. Crawford shot him another look of frustration and worry before he turned on his heel and walked back to the door. Merrick knew he was taking a chance, but it might be the only one he got.

"Release me," Merrick ordered in a low voice.

Merrick watched as Crawford's hand froze on the doorknob and he slowly turned around to face him. The human's face paled when he slowly rose from the bed and walked to the door of his cell. He stared back at the wide, dark brown eyes gaping back at him in shock.

"You speak... you understand...," Crawford stuttered.

"I learned your language... some," Merrick replied with a sharp nod. "Release me."

"I can't," Crawford whispered hoarsely. "Hell, I'm going to be lucky to get out of this alive as it is. If I release you, I'm dead. If Weston Wright doesn't kill me, Markham will. They even threatened my family if I said anything or tried to leave."

"Then help me," Merrick demanded.

"Didn't you just hear what I said?" Crawford asked in frustration. "If I so much as lift a finger to help you get away, not only am I dead, but so is my girl. That was made very clear the first night you were brought in."

"Call a number for me, then," Merrick insisted in a low voice. "The human can protect your family. He can send you and your female to a place where neither of these men can harm you."

Crawford gave a bitter laugh and shook his head. "Are you fucking kidding me? I did my research on these guys after they threatened me! Unless you can send me and Becky to another planet, there isn't a fucking rock on Earth where they won't hunt us down," he retorted.

"You would not be on your world," Merrick murmured in a low voice. "You would be on mine."

Crawford swallowed and paled. Merrick knew he had taken the human by surprise with his comment. It was a risk, but it was one he had to take if he was to get free.

"You... you aren't shitting me, are you?" Crawford whispered. "You really are a fucking alien."

"Yes," Merrick answered, staring intently into Crawford's eyes. "I know that they intend to kill you. Weston has joked about it when they do their tests on me. They do not realize I can understand them."

Merrick didn't think it was possible for the human to get any paler than he had been, but he did. He actually swayed for a moment before a flash of anger ignited in the depths of his dark eyes. He knew the moment the human made the decision to help him. His eyes followed Crawford's hand as he reached into his pocket and pulled out a small piece of paper and a pen.

"You said that there was a human that could protect Becky and me? Do you really think that? Do you think he could send us somewhere that we would be safe?" Crawford demanded in a harsh voice.

"Yes," Merrick replied calmly.

"Who is he?"

A smile curved Merrick's lips as he returned Crawford's intense stare. His fingers curled around the cold, steel bars. Finally... finally, the Goddess had heard his plea and answered him.

"Cosmos Raines," Merrick said. "You can reach him at this number."

* * *

Merrick sat back a few minutes later on the bed. A sense of expectancy filled him as he watched the door quietly close behind Crawford. Pulling one leg up, he uncurled his left hand again so he could touch the intricate pattern in the center. He closed his eyes and he concentrated on the face of the female. Opening his mind, he waited for the connection born of their bond to connect him with her.

A satisfied smile curved his lips when he felt the link between them connect. He could feel the confusion, fear, and worry coursing through her. He wished that he could hold her and reassure her that she needn't feel that way. Suddenly, her thoughts cleared and he could 'hear' the question resonating through her mind as if she was standing in front of him.

What the...? A clear picture of the same pattern that graced his palm formed in his mind.

The marking shows you have found your bond mate, he answered in a soft, whispered thought.

What... What is a bond mate? She hesitantly thought back.

Merrick could feel the trembling of fear in her thoughts. Frustration gnawed at him. He hated that he could not be there with her. Resentment tempered his response to her.

You are my bond mate. It means you belong to me! Tell me your name, he ordered.

He sent the demand more forcefully than he intended. A sense of regret filled him when he felt her instinctively flinch at the harsh projection of his thoughts. He had forgotten to ask Crawford for her name before he left. Now, he desperately needed it. It was almost as if he knew her name, it would give him the lifeline he needed to remain sane until Cosmos could send a team to free him.

Merrick leaned forward and clenched his fists to keep from howling in rage when nothing but silence met his demand. He tried pushing his thoughts into her head again, but it was as if she was no longer there. Pausing, he drew in a deep breath and released it. It took several minutes before he felt her tentatively reach out to him again. When he met her halfway, she hesitated, but didn't withdraw.

Who are you? She whispered in a small voice. *How can I hear you?*

I am Merrick Ta'Duran, Leader of the Eastern Mountain Clan on my home world of Baade, he replied in a soothing voice. *What is your name?*

I'm... I'm Addie, she replied. *I don't feel so good. I'm going to sleep now.*

Sleep well, Addie, Merrick murmured. "Sleep well, my beautiful, green-eyed mate," he repeated, twisting to lie back on the bed.

Chapter 5
Cosmos Raines Industries: Houston, Texas

Rose tiredly rubbed her brow. She glanced at where Trudy was sleeping on the couch in their thirtieth floor office of Cosmos Raines Industries building in Houston, Texas. A smile tugged at her lips and she shook her head.

When Trudy slept, she slept in utter abandon. She was lying on her stomach, her face was buried in the pillow, one arm was over her head, while the other was off the couch. She didn't know why she hadn't pulled out the bed in the other room that was built into the wall. Cosmos had it installed after he came in and discovered Trudy passed out on the floor and her on the couch a couple of years ago. They had worked eight straight days in order to track down a serial killer.

Looking at her childhood friend, no one would know that Trudy had a gift for solving complex puzzles with just a glance. Trudy's skills at seeing patterns, combined with her skills at reading people and identifying the smallest detail made them a dynamic team. They used to drive everyone nuts when they were younger. They were often compared to Sherlock Holmes and Watson.

"Not that we are all that old," Rose whispered, turning back to the screen. "I just wish those bastards would stay in one spot long enough to catch them."

"What?" Trudy mumbled, lifting her head.

"Go back to sleep. I'm just talking to myself again," Rose called over her shoulder.

"'Kay," Trudy replied, burying her face in the pillow again.

Rose chuckled and turned back to replay the video files they had downloaded. There had to be detail they were missing. The last three times she and Trudy had pieced together where those jerks had taken the MA, her and Trudy's nickname for the Missing Alien, they had been a day late and a dollar short. It was royally pissing her off.

Avery was going to chew their asses out if they missed getting him this next time. A shiver ran through Rose as she thought of her boss. Avery was a great boss, but she didn't like it when things didn't come together the way she thought they should.

Rose turned as the door to the office that she and Trudy shared suddenly opened. She fought the urge to roll her eyes when she saw who was standing in the doorway. Instead, she glanced into Trudy's sleepy ones and saw the amusement in them.

Think of the devil and she walks in unannounced, Rose thought as she stiffly rose out of the chair in front of the bank of computers.

"Rose, I have some help for you," Avery said, glancing at where Trudy was slowly shifting so she could sit up. "How is it going?"

"Great... Frustrating," Rose reluctantly admitted. "I don't know who Avilov hired, but he is one smart bastard."

"Then, it is a good thing you'll have some extra help," Avery commented as she stepped to the side and nodded her head. "Runt, this is Rose…"

"Caine," Runt muttered. "You have your Doctorate in multiple computer based programming languages and your ability to write code and understand advanced algorithms are pretty good."

"Pretty good…," Trudy replied, glancing at the stony expression on Rose's face before she looked at the young girl standing in the doorway looking at the floor. "Ouch, just pretty good? That hurt, Rose."

"And you are Amelia Thomas, aka The Runt," Rose retorted, folding her arms across her chest and staring at the suddenly closed face. "You've hacked into hundreds of computer systems throughout the world making you one of the most prolific hackers under the age of sixteen. You've also emptied the bank accounts of more than one illegal operation, making you a liability. You were able to escape detection until you tried to hack into Raines Industries two years ago. We caught you running a concentrated loop of programming in an effort to slip through our security systems."

"She did a wonderful job of it, too. I absolutely love her coding and she was doing such a superb job shutting down all of those awful men. I was just worried about her, which is why I sent her the invitation to come try to break into Cosmos' company. I knew he would want her as part of the team and she would be safe under Avery's watchful eye," a voice suddenly said. "By the way, hello, sweetheart. How have you been doing? I've missed you the past few months."

*　*　*

Runt lifted her head, a slight smile lifted the corner of her mouth at the familiar voice before it died and she looked back down at the floor. Pulling her oversized coat closer around her, she hugged her waist. She didn't want to be here. Closed in places made her nervous, especially closed in places with people she didn't trust... which was everyone.

She pulled her cold hands inside the sleeves of the coat. There was only one 'person' in the world she really trusted, and that was RITA, Cosmos Raines artificial intelligence computer program. It was weird, but RITA reminded her of her mom. A brief flash of pain swept through Runt as she remembered the beautiful woman who had loved her for being her, not because of what she could do.

"Hey, RITA," Runt muttered.

"Would you like to come take a look at what Rose and Trudy are working on? I think you would find it fascinating," RITA encouraged.

"No, I want to leave," she replied in a suddenly desperate voice. "What do you guys want from me, anyway? You've got better hacks than me here."

A shiver of unease ran through her when the tall, slender woman with icy eyes looked down at her with an intense, determined gaze. The woman had been searching for her, which is why RITA hadn't 'heard' from her. She had been hiding and staying off the grid until a couple of days ago.

It had taken almost a dozen men to finally block all of her escape routes. She didn't understand what this woman or Cosmos Raines would want from her. She hadn't been just saying they had better hackers than her. Rose Caine and Trudy Wilson were some of the smartest in the world.

Deep down, Runt knew she was as good as they were. She had always been more at home in front of a computer than anywhere else. That had been obvious when she started kindergarten and had hacked into the school's network when the teacher logged her in under her account. The school psychologist, and the doctor the psychologist insisted her mom take her to, had diagnosed her as having high functioning autism. They recommended she be placed in special classes.

Runt had diagnosed the two doctors as being idiots. Fortunately, her mom pulled her from the public school to home school her. Unfortunately, her mom had stayed with her dad. Once her father realized what she could do, he had taken advantage of it. Deep down, Runt knew that the activities her dad had her doing were behind her mom's death.

Personally, it didn't matter to her what anyone thought about her; it never had and never would. Heck, if she had her way, the world would be populated with more RITA's. As far as she was concerned, humanity could die off and she wouldn't give a damn. She could count the number of good ones on one hand with four fingers still free. Humans were cruel, evil beings.

Well, most of them, she reluctantly admitted as she thought of the old man that she had brought food to over the past year. He had been nice to her.

Bert lived near the warehouse where she had been living until a few months ago. She hadn't seen him since the night her life had turned upside down. Bert had befriended her and made her feel needed. There wasn't another person on Earth that she would give two cents to save, if she had that much in her pocket.

The sudden dark image of another figure from that night flashed through her mind and a sense of panic unexpectedly swept through her. Four months before she had been following a lead about some bad-asses from overseas when some men had taken over the warehouse where she had been living since her dad died.

The men had brought a really beautiful woman there. Runt knew immediately there was something different about the woman. The woman didn't act scared like the other girls Runt had seen on the streets. The men had taken the woman inside the warehouse.

She had been about to sneak through a hole in the metal framing when two of the guards that had come with the other men saw her. One of them had grabbed her and thrown her down. That was when the third man came out of nowhere.

"I have to get out of here," Runt muttered, pushing the memory away as she remembered him touching her. "I've got to go before he finds me." She didn't realize that she had spoken aloud until Avery asked her who she was talking about.

"Before who finds you?" The woman named Avery asked in a quiet, soothing voice.

"Derik 'Tag Krell Manok. He has been searching for Amelia," RITA replied before Runt could. "She is his bond mate."

"Holy shit," Rose and Trudy whispered, looking at Runt in surprise.

"Just fucking great!" Avery muttered in aggravation. "Like we need any more drama going on."

"Who is Derik 'Tag Krell Manok and what is a bond mate?" Runt nervously asked, glancing up at the three women staring at her in the sudden silence.

Chapter 6

Addie groaned and buried her face in the pillow as a shaft of sunlight streamed through the narrow slit in the curtains covering her bedroom window. She finally turned her head to glance at the clock on the nightstand. It was almost eight-thirty.

You are hurt? A deep voice asked.

"What the...!"

Addie jerked as the voice that she thought she had dreamed about flowed through her mind. Turning, she sat up and glanced frantically around her bedroom. Nope, it was her room. She tilted her head, focusing to see if she could miraculously hear, but there was nothing but the same silence.

"Who are you?" She whispered, pulling her legs up to her chest.

Merrick Ta'Duran, Leader of the Eastern Mountain Clan, he replied in a soothing voice.

Unfortunately, the soothing voice wasn't doing its job. The goose bumps that rose along Addie's exposed arms had nothing to do with the cooler air of her apartment. Addie swallowed as she pressed a hand to her head. Images of the man in the cage from last night flashed through her mind. She hadn't dreamed it.

"What are you?" She asked suddenly as she remembered the man's glowing eyes and elongated canines.

I am a Prime warrior, he responded.

"What the hell is a Prime warrior? How can you talk to me in my head? What is going on? Why do they have you in a cage?" Addie growled in annoyance born more out of fear than anger.

It is a long story, he reluctantly replied.

Then give me an abbreviated version, Addie retorted as she lowered her legs and tucked her hair behind her right ear.

She rolled her eyes at her image in the mirror on her dresser. She looked like an insane banshee this morning! Her hair was sticking up all over the place, her left cheek had wrinkles from the pillow, and she was glaring at her reflection in frustration.

I am from a distant world called Baade. I was captured several months ago during a mission. As my bond mate, I am able to communicate with you. It is the way of my people. It allows me to know if you are in danger so I can protect you, Merrick explained.

"So, you are telling me you're an alien from another world?" Addie asked in disbelief tinged with dismay. "If you haven't noticed, I don't need your protection. If anything, it looks like you are the one that needs the protecting. And what the hell is a bond mate?

It means you belong to me, Merrick grunted. *I will be free soon. Others will come for me. When I am, I will come for you. You must stay away from here until then. You are in danger.*

Okay, let's get a few things straight before you get out of my head, Addie thought in irritation as she pushed the covers back and swung her legs over the side of the bed. *First, I am not your bond mate. Which, if you think it means what I think you are thinking it means, you can just forget it! Second, I am not the one in the cage, you are... That means, you are the one in danger, not me. I can help you. I can call the police and they can come and rescue you.*

No! No more of your people must know of my existence. It is too dangerous. Your world is not ready to know that others exist outside of your world, Merrick pushed through.

Addie winced at the force of his thoughts. It was almost the equivalent of someone 'shouting'. Her mind swept through a wide spectrum of solutions, trying to figure out a way to save him.

She *so* did not have time for this, but she couldn't just ignore it either. It was obvious that he needed help. After several long seconds, she had to admit that he was right about no one else knowing. People would freak out worse than she was planning to do once she got him out of her head!

Aliens! God, I totally don't need to have the world go to hell right now. I am so close to finally getting my life where I want it. She thought before she flushed at her selfish thoughts. *You said that others of your kind would come for you. Why haven't they come yet?* Addie asked in frustration as she walked over to the thermostat and turned it up a little.

The people who hold me prisoner move me to different places every few weeks, Merrick reluctantly admitted.

So, what is different now? Addie asked pointedly. *Besides that I know about you. Is it possible for me to contact them? I can tell them where you are.*

No!

Ouch! You don't have to shout, Addie grumbled, pressing her trembling fingers to her forehead as she walked into the small kitchenette. *Why not?*

I will not endanger you, Merrick insisted. *I have another who will contact my friends.*

What, so you would endanger someone else? Addie asked with a touch of skepticism. *Who is going to help you?*

The guard who found you last night, Merrick admitted before a low snarl escaped him. *I will not be able to talk to you for a while.*

Why? Addie asked, pausing as she lifted the carton of orange juice to her mouth. *What's going on?*

They come for me again, he bit out.

Who comes for you? Addie demanded, setting the container in her hand down on the counter. *Who is coming for you? Merrick?*

"Damn it!" Addie muttered, bowing her head when she felt the familiar silence surround her again.

* * *

"The tests coming back are inconclusive," Dr. Margaret Rockman argued, glaring at the two men standing at the entrance to the room. "I need more time."

"You'll have to finish the tests at the Reno lab," Weston stated. "He has been here too long."

"How do you expect me to get any work done if I have to keep interrupting it?" Margaret demanded, pulling off her gloves and throwing them in the trash can.

"You have his blood, what more do you need?" Weston demanded, glancing at Merrick's still figure.

"You are such an ignorant ass, you wouldn't understand," Margaret replied, looking at Merrick. "His ability to heal is unbelievable. I cut a two inch incision across his forearm yesterday and it has already healed until I can barely tell where it was! That is just the start. The bone and muscle scans, not to mention the endurance tests, prove he has increased speed and strength. I need to get a sample of his bone marrow."

"You can cut him into tiny pieces when we get to the Reno lab," Markham replied in a sharp tone. "That will be the last chance you have to get what you need, Dr. Rockman. I've been ordered to terminate him. My client is not impressed with your findings to date considering that the last four facilities he owns has been shut down. The cost has exceeded your lab rat's value."

"I need more time!" Margaret snapped.

"You're out of it," Markham replied dismissively as he turned and walked out of the room.

"Asshole," Margaret muttered under her breath as she glanced at Merrick's inert figure strapped to the exam table. "It will take years to study him. I need him alive, not dead."

"You'd better figure out a way to clone him if you want to study him," Weston said as he turned away. "That's the only way you'll have anything left after Markham gets done with him, Doc."

Margaret glared at Weston Wright's back as he walked out of the door. Fury at the constant interruptions, lack of equipment, and fragmented time frames she was given to study the huge male burned through her. Her gaze returned to the still face of the male on the table. A calculating look suddenly glinted in her eyes.

"Perhaps not a clone," she murmured as she ran her eyes down over his body. "But something that I can keep without the others knowing about. It might not be completely alien like you, but close enough."

Margaret looked up at the two guards that stood in the doorway. She stepped to the side so that they could wheel the exam table back into the cage. Her mouth curved upward. Now, all she needed to do was find the right enticement.

Chapter 7

Will you be quiet! I need to concentrate, Addie growled silently, staring down at the paper in front of her. *Has anyone ever told you, you think too much?*

The low sound of tired masculine laughter echoed in her head, pulling another soft groan from her. She glanced up and saw her Anatomy professor looking at her. She gave him a weak smile, before lowering her head.

Her hair fell forward, screening her face as she gazed down at the final exam paper in front of her. For the past two hours, she had been having a silent argument in her head with the man she saw last night.

Merrick, he insisted. *Say my name.*

Correction, I've been listening to him constantly try to boss me around for the past two hours, she grimaced when he repeated his name... for the hundredth time.

I know your name! She snapped back when his chuckle echoed through her mind again. *I have to finish this test. Once it is done, I promise I'll talk to you, okay? Now, will you just shut up for a little while? This is important and I can't concentrate with you growling and snarling at me.*

You should not have shut me out, Merrick retorted in irritation. *I am your bond mate. You should never close me off.*

I wasn't the one who shut you out first, remember? Besides, I was driving and didn't want to get myself killed. Traffic is brutal in the mid-mornings. And for goodness sake, will you quit calling me that! I am NOT your bond mate, Addie responded forcefully. *Now, will you just let me finish my test? It is my last class. Once I'm done, I'll talk to you again.*

Only if you promise me that you will give up your ludicrous plan! Merrick insisted. *You must not come here.*

I'm supposed to work tonight. If I don't, they will get suspicious. Listen, my plan will work. You'll see, Addie insisted, glancing up at her teacher again, who was frowning at her. *I've got to go. My teacher is giving me a nasty look. I swear, I'll be back in a few.*

No, Addie, Merrick repeated. *Please... I cannot protect you yet.*

Don't you worry about me... Merrick, Addie said, trying to ease his mind. *I've got a plan and I can help you. I know I can do this.*

Addie sighed and blinked several times when she felt him pull away from her. Tears burned her eyes when she thought of the tiredness and pain in his voice. She suspected he had no idea that she could hear or feel it, but she could. Whatever had happened to him earlier when he cut her off must have been bad.

Releasing her breath, she focused on the paper in front of her. She pushed everything away, except for what she had to do at this moment. It didn't take her long to finish the test. She had been studying like crazy for it for weeks and Anatomy was one of her favorite classes so she felt fairly confident when she stood up twenty minutes later to hand it to her teacher.

Sighing her thanks, she quickly left the room. The moment she was out the door, she picked up speed until she was practically running. Waving her hand at a car that stopped to let her pass, she crossed to the car park and to her car. Pressing the remote, she climbed in and quickly started it. She had a lot to do before she showed up for work tonight.

* * *

"Merrick, are you there?" Addie thought anxiously as she opened the door to her apartment.

Tossing her keys onto the counter, she glanced at the clock. Ted would be leaving for Keiser soon. She would need to get the set of lock picks from him before he left.

Yes, Merrick finally replied. *You have finished your exam?*

"Yeah," Addie replied with a sigh.

You did well? He asked.

Addie rolled her eyes. After so many years with nothing but her own thoughts in her head, it was kind of weird to be having a conversation with someone else in it. If talking to an alien in her head wasn't freaky enough, the fact that he was asking how her final exam went just added to the unreality of the situation.

"I'm pretty sure I aced it," she replied. "It was my favorite class."

What are you learning? He murmured.

"Anatomy," Addie responded as she stepped out of her apartment and across the hall to Pam and Ted's. Knocking, she waited impatiently for Ted to answer. "Listen, do you swear you won't hurt me and that your people aren't here to take over the Earth and all that?"

The deep laughter that echoed through her was filled with amusement, not menace. Addie was pretty confident that anyone that sounded like that couldn't be bad. There was no 'evil madman' in it, just pure delight.

No, we have no desire to invade your world, Merrick said. *I swear on my life.*

"Oh, okay. Hold on a second, I'll be right back," Addie muttered when the door opened.

"Hi, Addie," Ted greeted her in a startled voice. He quickly signed to her. "Is everything okay?"

Addie smiled reassuringly at Ted. Signing, she asked if she could 'borrow' his lock pick set. It wasn't the first time she had to use it. One of her nephews had locked her bathroom door the last time her sister Alisha visited. Since it was the only one, it had been imperative to get it open.

Ted grinned. He nodded and turned back into his and Pam's apartment. Addie followed him inside and watched as he bent to lift his tool bag. She looked around, puzzled, when she didn't see Pam.

"Where is Pam?" Addie asked in a husky voice.

Ted turned so he was facing her. "She went to her mom and dad's for the week. She's expecting, and wanted to tell them in person."

"That is awesome! Congratulations!" Addie replied with a grin.

She impulsively stepped forward and wrapped her arms around Ted's waist to give him a brief hug. A surprised gasp escaped her when she heard a low, menacing growl ricochet through her head. Pulling back, she blinked up at Ted before releasing an uneasy laugh.

Knock it off, Addie pushed out, trying to cover her discomfort.

You should not touch another male, Merrick retorted, disgruntedly.

Ted is my best friend! I've known him and his wife, Pam, since I was a kid, Addie snapped silently. *They are having a baby. Of course, I'd give him a hug.*

I... apologize, Merrick finally responded.

Yeah, you should, Addie muttered. *Just... chill for a minute more.*

"So, did you lock yourself out of the bathroom again?" Ted teased before he turned to pick up the small plastic case holding a wide variety of picks. "You can hold onto this set," he added, holding it out to her. "I don't need it back any time soon. I bought a really nice set to replace it."

Addie nodded as she read his lips. Signing her thanks, she turned to head back to her apartment. She paused in surprise when she felt a hand on her arm. Turning, she looked back at Ted.

"Are you okay?" He signed.

"Of course," Addie replied. "Why?"

"I don't know," he said, shifting from one foot to the other. "You seem a little pre-occupied."

"I had my final exam today," Addie said with a shrug. "I'm just worried about how I did."

"Oh, okay," Ted replied with a nod. "I'll see you later tonight at work."

"See you later," Addie responded, thankfully escaping.

It is too dangerous. I told you, I gave the guard information to call for help, Merrick insisted.

Well, think of this as Plan B, in case he doesn't, Addie silently retorted, stepping back into her apartment and closing the door. *I don't know what happened to you this morning, but you can't take much more.*

You are the most...

A chuckle escaped Addie at the obvious curse that fluttered through her mind. She didn't care. It was a good plan... and not that dangerous, at least for her. She would do her job. When she got to his level, she would slip the set of lock picks she had borrowed from Ted to him.

It would take seconds at the most. She would be in and out. After that, it was up to him. Well, sort of. He would need a distraction to help him get out of the building. She was still working on that part of the plan.

And that is why you should not be doing this! Merrick's voice interrupted her thoughts again.

Addie crossed her eyes and stuck her tongue out. Growing up with a hoard of older siblings led one to use a lot of creative faces when you didn't want your parents to see the numerous silent battles. Addie's repertoire had grown significantly since she lost her hearing.

"You need to just either help me figure out an idea or keep out of my head. This is going to be scary enough as it is without you making it worse," she complained. "If I get the tools to you, do you think you can undo the locks?"

YESSSS! His voice hissed back in annoyance.

Addie winced at the heat behind the single word. You don't have to be so… forget it. Once you get out, follow the path I'll include with the tools. I'll leave my keycard with you as well. Once you reach the back parking lot, I'll be waiting. You jump in the back, I drive us through the gate while you call your friends to pick you up. I drop you off and we both get our lives back. You go home and I don't have to mop anymore floors. Problem solved."

You forget about the cameras, Weston and Markham, and Dr. Rockman, Merrick replied in a surly tone.

"I told you, I'll cause a distraction," Addie pointed out as she packed her backpack for work later that night. "The bad guys won't be there. It will be late. They'll be home in bed… I hope."

Addie winced again when she realized the last two words slipped past her before she could stop them. She was learning two things about this way of communication. First, she could close him out, but it wasn't easy and not for very long. Second, if she didn't want him to know what she was thinking, she better not think it in the first place.

That is why you must not do this, he growled.

"Has anyone ever told you, you sound like a broken record?" Addie muttered under her breath. "I've got this. I can do this. In and out, simple, fast, and run like hell. I used to do it all the time to my older brothers. I can do this."

Silence greeted her words. Addie tentatively reached out trying to see if she could find the strange feeling that she had begun to recognize that he was there. Yep, he was still there. Silent, stubborn, aggravating, hard-headed...

Did I list stubborn? She wondered as she slung the backpack over her shoulder and headed for the door.

* * *

Yes, you mentioned it already, Merrick chuckled in response before he pulled away when she told him she needed to focus on driving again.

A sigh escaped Merrick as he laid tiredly back on the bed. He had woken with a thunderous headache. He didn't know what Dr. Rockman had done to him, but his head felt as if it was about to explode.

It may have been the drug they used to sedate him. This was one of the first times where they had sedated him and returned him back to his cell before he had woken. A sense of unease and urgency was building inside him. This time had been different. He hated not knowing what was done to him while he was unconscious.

As much as he detested Addie's plan, he had to admit it might be his only chance of escape. He relaxed, forcing himself to take a deep breath and calm his mind. His thoughts turned to Addie. She was an unusual female, much like those he had met back on Prime in the Council's chambers.

A smile curved his lips and he closed his eyes as he remembered the human sisters, Tink, Hannah, and Tansy Bell. Each were different from the other, but strong in a surprising way. The more he learned about them, the more intrigued he had become. The fact that he had also found his own bond mate among this species both thrilled and concerned him.

He was thrilled to find Addie, there was no doubts about that. In his mind, he remembered her curvy figure. She wasn't tiny, like J'kar's mate Tink, or lean like Borj's mate, Hannah.

No, Addie had a fuller figure with hips that made his hands itch to hold and breasts... a soft groan escaped him as he felt his body react to imagines playing through his mind.

Knock it off, Addie suddenly interrupted. *You almost made me run into the back of the car in front of me! Add dirty mind to the list of descriptions for you.*

I am sorry, Merrick replied sheepishly.

No, you're not, Addie chuckled. *I grew up with three older brothers. Knowing what they are thinking is not something I ever wanted to experience. So, I think it is best to keep some things to yourself. And, for your information, my hips and breasts are not THAT big.*

I think they are perfect. From what I have seen, he added.

I am blocking you out before I have an accident, Addie replied in exasperation. *You'd better be thinking of how you are going to get free rather than what my body looks like.*

True, but it is not as enjoyable, Merrick teased.

Whatever, Addie retorted before he felt her slam the wall up between them, shutting him out.

That was something else he was learning about her, she had a sense of humor that both amused and fascinated him. She was also stubborn and not in the least intimidated by him, or didn't appear to be from her determination to help him. And that, is what concerned him.

He knew that the humans would not think twice about hurting Addie if she was caught. Frustration ate at him that he didn't know if the guard he had taken a chance on would truly help him or not . The after effects of the drug used on him and the continued lack of rest wore on him.

Breathing deeply, he closed his eyes. He would gather what rest he could before tonight. It took a while, but he finally felt the easing of the pounding in his head and slipped into a light doze.

* * *

Merrick blinked and turned his head when the door opened almost three hours later. He watched as Crawford stepped into the room. The male was pale as he glanced nervously toward the door he just closed.

"Listen, I… I have my girl making the call," Crawford said in a low, urgent tone as he stepped just close enough to the bars that Merrick wouldn't be able to reach him should he try. "It was too dangerous for me to make it. Becky is going to buy a disposal cell phone at the grocery store. I had to… I had to tell her a little of what was going on so she would be careful. She's going to get some cash and go to a place outside of town until your friends come and take us away, but she'll make the call tonight."

Merrick rolled off the bunk and to his feet. Stepping closer to the bars, he watched in silence as Crawford glanced uneasily behind him again. There was something the male wasn't telling him. He was too tense.

"What is happening?" Merrick demanded, wrapping his fingers around the bar.

"I'm not sure," Crawford replied. "I came in late to work this afternoon. Listen, I want you to know I didn't know what was going on here."

"You said that before," Merrick retorted in a low voice. "What are you not telling me?"

Crawford swallowed, glancing over his shoulder. "I got notice…"

Crawford turned and paled when the door suddenly opened behind him. Weston and Markham stood in the doorway. Merrick's eyes darkened and his lip curled back in a snarl as Weston raised the pistol in his hand and fired it.

Merrick reached out, grabbing Crawford as he fell back against the bars of the cage. He slowly lowered the male to the floor as Crawford's eyes glazed with pain, fear, and resignation. Rage and regret poured through him as the dying man turned to look at him.

"You promised," Crawford whispered. "Becky... You prom..."

Merrick drew in a deep breath before turning his blazing eyes on the two men standing in the doorway. Rising to his feet, he straightened his shoulders and clenched his fists as Weston and Markham stepped into the room. He watched and waited to see what would happen next.

"So, you speak," Markham observed calmly. "I suspected that you understood what was being said."

Merrick refused to respond. There was nothing to say to either male. He could only hope that whatever was to happen did so quickly, before Addie was endangered.

Addie, you must stay away from here, Merrick pushed out as a sense of panic began to build in him.

Too late, came her soft reply. *I'm already upstairs cleaning.*

You need to leave NOW! Merrick ordered.

Why? Came her hesitant response. *Merrick, what's wrong?*

Weston and Markham are here, he replied. *Weston just killed the guard who was to help me.*

Oh my god, Addie responded in horror after a few, long seconds of silence. *I'm leaving. I have to call for help, Merrick. You said he was going to help you. You have to let me do that now.*

There is a human called Cosmos Raines, Merrick said urgently. *Tell him what has happened. His number is...* His voice died as he jerked back in shock.

Merrick? Merrick! Please... Merrick?

Merrick tried to answer, but the impact of the tranquilizers striking him in the chest and shoulder knocked him backwards. The painful burning from the new sedative they were using on him exploded like fire in his veins. The powerful drug took his breath away for a moment as it swept through him. He crumbled when another dart embedded into his upper left thigh and his leg went numb.

Addie... run, he pushed out before the drug overpowered him.

Chapter 8

Addie pushed her hair back from her face and stood frozen in front of one of the windows overlooking the parking lot far below. She waited impatiently for Merrick to finish giving her the information she needed. She jerked in surprise when a flash of pain exploded through her before it disappeared.

Addie... run!

Fear made her clumsy as she twisted around. Pulling her cell phone out of her back pocket, she pushed it down the front of her bra. A precautionary trick she had learned from a safety class at school.

She knocked against the cleaning cart as she pulled open the door to the office she was in and stepped into the narrow hallway. Her lips parted in surprise when she saw the elevator doors open through the clear glass double doors in front of the office at the same time the guard that had been with Crawford last night stepped out of it.

Their eyes connected and Addie knew that it wasn't a coincidence that he had suddenly decided to check this floor. Turning, she began running in the opposite direction as fast as she could. The knowledge that she was in danger, and the fact the guard had to use his security card to open the doors, gave her a slight edge as she rounded the corner. There was another door leading out into the main section of the floor further up the corridor. Her fear made her clumsy and it took several tries before her key card disengaged the lock on the door.

Addie had just pushed open the door when a cry escaped her as the guard's hard body hit her from behind. The force of the impact drove her through the open door and into the outside hallway. The breath was knocked out of her when the guard landed on top of her. Pure panic drove her to push him up enough that she could roll beneath him. Bringing her knee up, she connected with his groin in a savage blow.

"Shit!" The guard hissed out as he rolled onto his back away from her and grabbed his crotch. "Son-of-a-bitch!"

Addie scrambled to her feet and took off down the hallway to the stairwell exit. With a shaking hand, she swiped her keycard across the access point, so the alarm wouldn't sound. Shoving the door open, she gripped the handrail to keep herself from falling as she missed the first step in her hurry to escape.

Her eyes flew to the wall after several floors. She was almost to the seventh floor. She had just turned onto the landing when the door next to her opened. A man she had never seen before stood in the doorway. Her eyes flew from his face to his hand.

Adrenaline burst through her when she saw the gun in it. Slamming her body against the door, she knocked him back into the hallway. The force and surprise of her attack knocked the gun from his hand and it fell to the floor in front of her.

Addie cursed when her right foot caught it and it went bouncing down the steps in front of her. She scrambled down after it as it skidded to a stop against the wall on the lower landing. Reaching for it, she fell to her hands and knees and slightly turned toward the upper landing when she felt the vibration of the door behind her as it banged open against the wall.

The gun fell limply from her fingers when she felt the touch of cold metal against her left temple. Shaking, she froze on the cold, hard concrete floor. Her eyes moved up the stairs to the face of the furious man coming down the steps toward her. Still, she didn't move for fear the man holding the gun at her temple would pull the trigger.

She focused on the man's mouth as he spoke to the man next to her. He appeared to be arguing with him. Pushing against the overwhelming fright, she forced her mind to concentrate on the words he was forming.

"You should just fucking kill her!" The man was saying. "I thought you were planning on killing the bastard when we got to the next location." His lips still for a moment as he listened to whatever the other man was saying. "Fine, but he'll probably just kill her too."

Addie cried out in surprise when the man suddenly stepped forward and grabbed her forearms in a crushing grip. Jerking her to her feet, he savagely shook her before pushing her back against the wall and bent to pick up his gun. Checking it, he looked back at her again.

"You fucking blink wrong and you are dead, do you understand me?" The man asked.

"She can't hear you," the guard from behind him said. "The bitch is deaf."

"Then let's see if she understands this," the man said before he pressed the end of the gun to her forehead.

Addie closed her eyes and whimpered as she waited. It was only when she felt a stinging tap to her chin that her eyelashes fluttered open. Turning her gaze to the man who originally held the gun on her, she looked at him in confusion and terror.

She wished she hadn't when she suddenly felt like fainting. The cold, dead look was enough to make her want to. Unfortunately, the man refused to release her from his intense gaze so she could.

"Nod if you want to live," the man said.

Addie wasn't even aware that her head moved. The man's eyes narrowed as he held her gaze. A slow, menacing smile curved his lips as he studied her terrified face.

"He might not kill this one," he remarked. "Bring her and notify Rockman we have her another plaything to use for her experiments."

Addie's expression turned to confusion when she felt fingers tighten around her forearm. Her head whipped back and forth, trying to understand what was going on. She desperately reached for Merrick, hoping to feel that strange sensation.

Panic made her briefly resist the tug on her arm. Another husky cry of pain escaped her when the fingers tightened brutally to the point she was afraid the man would snap the bones in her arm. She stumbled into the guard when he stepped down the last step as she was pulled forward.

"What do you want me to do?" The guard asked.

"Clean up Crawford's body," the man with the icy, cold eyes ordered.

Merrick? Please… Answer me, Addie thought.

Her eyes followed the guard as he continued to walk past her. The fingers of her right hand curled into a fist. As long as she was alive, she had a chance of escaping. Pressing her hand to her stomach, she stumbled again as she clutched the prize she had taken from the guard's belt when he had passed.

Thank god for older brothers, she thought as she slipped the keys that had dangled loosely from his pocket into the waistband of her jeans.

* * *

"Rose," Trudy whispered, snapping her fingers to get her friend and partner's attention.

"How can I help you?" Trudy asked in the headset as Rose gave her a sharp nod.

"RITA, make sure you lock onto the caller's location," Rose muttered.

"No problem, dear. I'm already on it," RITA replied.

"A… A man named Merrick told my boyfriend if he called this number, you could help us… me," a low, shaky voice whispered. "He... He said you could protect us. Please… Please, help me. They… I think they might have done something to Bradley. He was supposed to call me over an hour ago. He said if he didn't that I needed to hide until you could help…

help me. I think they are after me now. There was a car following me earlier, but I lost whoever it was when I left my car in the parking lot at the grocery store. Please... Help us. I don't know what is happening. Please... Please."

"Do you know where Merrick is?" Trudy asked, looking at the screen in front of her as it scrolled through dozens of locations before narrowing on the city of Portland, Oregon. She covered the microphone with her hand and turned to Rose. "Anything?"

"Just a few more seconds," Rose replied. "RITA, lock into the satellite at the following coordinates.

"Yes, I'm watching the building now, hoping I will see Bradley," the woman on the other end replied. "He works at Keiser..."

"Institute of Technology and Research, Portland, Oregon division," Rose finished. "Scanning personnel and security video now. Whatever they have there, they don't want anyone taking a peek. It has some major security coding in it. RITA, can you find us a back door without them knowing we are there?"

"Of course," RITA, Cosmos' Raines AI software replied in a dry tone. "They may be good, Rose, but I'm somewhat spectacular if you ask me."

Rose's soft snort echoed in the upper rooms of Cosmos' Enterprises. Spectacular was too mild an adjective to describe RITA. Rose had been shocked when she discovered that RITA wasn't really one of Cosmos Raines' brilliant inventions, but that of his roommate, Jasmine, aka Tinker, Bell and her mother, Tilly. After meeting both women, Rose could appreciate RITA's sense of humor and almost motherly attitude.

While the computer software and the highly secretive server that contained it might have the technical name 'Really Intelligent Technical Assistant', there was no way RITA could be described as anything else, but futuristic. Her ability to learn, adapt, and process information was mind boggling.

"I have the location," Rose whispered, patching an alert through to the advanced team for deployment before alerting Avery. "Avery, we have a location. There is a woman on the phone that says Merrick gave her boyfriend this number. Yes, Team One and Four have been ordered to deploy. We'll be in the air in ten minutes."

"RITA, keep us connected as long as you can," Rose ordered. "Are there any satellites feeds available?"

"I have two satellites within range in three minutes," RITA replied. "I've accessed video surveillance cameras around Keiser and am uploading to each Teams command center. I'll track any incoming and outgoing vehicles within ten blocks and expand the search outward."

Trudy turned in her chair and rose, pulling off the headset. "She hung up. All she knew was that her boyfriend, Bradley Crawford, worked as a security guard for Keiser for the past six months. She said he had been extremely tense about something for a couple of weeks. Last night he told her to call this number and tell whoever answered, that Merrick said we would protect them. She couldn't tell me anything else and sounded scared out of her mind," she explained as she took the Kevlar vest Rose held out.

"The helicopter is ready," Rose said with a nod. "Let's get moving. Team One was on standby in California. They should be there with the next hour. RITA has all cameras in the area under her control."

"Shit," Trudy muttered. "Homeland is going to be calling Cosmos again."

"Not this time," Rose chuckled. "We have the President's permission."

"Thank goodness," Trudy said as she stepped into the private elevator. "I hope that means Lady Luck is on our side this time."

The doors to the elevator closed on the two women. Neither of them noticed the silent figure standing near the door leading to the bedroom attached to the office. Runt stepped into the room and quickly walked over to the computer panel. Within minutes, she was pulling up the video that RITA was looking at and coding her own search software into the computer.

"You really are extremely good at this, Amelia," RITA observed with a gentle voice. "Cosmos and his team could really use your skills."

"I don't like people, RITA," Runt replied. "They won't make it in time. Look at the blueprints. There is an underground system. That is how they'll move him. There are no cameras there. They must have known it could be hacked. Have you managed to get into their security system?"

"Yes, they have pulled the tapes and shut down the main power grid. From what I can see, the hard drives were removed an hour ago, according to the logs," RITA replied. "Still, there may be something that can give us a clue to where they may take him next."

"Uh-huh," Runt replied in a distracted voice as her fingers flew across the keyboard.

She drew in a swift breath when she found what she was looking for, a picture from inside Cosmos Raines warehouse home. She had been running the secondary search embedded in the first one. A moment of sweet triumph swept through her when she realized that RITA hadn't caught the simple, but effective code.

Pressing the print button, Runt printed the image of the male on the screen. She quickly erased her search history before rising out of the seat. Pulling the colorful print off of the laser printer, she gazed at the intense eyes and rigid features of the man from the warehouse that had been haunting her for the past four months.

"You know, if you had just asked, I would have given you the information," RITA's soft voice echoed in the room.

"Where...," Runt paused, gazing down at the image for a few seconds before she carefully folded it and slipped it into her pocket. "What is a bond mate?"

"It means you are his, Amelia," RITA responded in a gentle voice. "You are his world, his only focus, his wife on his world."

"His… world?" Runt whispered, staring blankly at the computer console and pulling her tattered jacket closer around her. "What is he?"

"He is a Prime warrior from another planet," RITA said. "He will stop at nothing to find you, sweetheart. You are young, though. He will not do anything until you are older."

"You mean… He's an alien?" Runt whispered in disbelief.

"Yes," RITA said. "They really aren't so bad. I've uploaded another version of myself into their computer system and I have to say, they are a hot group of hunks. I swear RITA2's circuits were practically sizzling!"

"I don't care how hot they are! I don't want anything to do with anyone," Runt muttered, bowing her head as a blush heated her cheeks.

"Where are you going?" RITA asked as Runt turned toward the elevator that Rose and Trudy had left in.

"To get something to eat from the cafeteria downstairs," Runt replied. "I'm hungry."

"The cooks downstairs are some of the best in the world," RITA replied cheerfully. "You should try their cookies. I hear Rose constantly raving about them."

"Thanks," Runt mumbled, stepping into the elevator and pressing the basement level.

What she didn't add was that she would pack some of the food and keep going. She knew RITA would have picked up a lie, so she told the truth... just not all of it. It was time to disappear again. Only this time, it would be permanent.

There was no way she was going to let some guy claim her as his bond mate. She saw what happened when a man held power over a woman. No matter how much her mom tried, she had been too weak to leave her dad.

That weakness ended up killing her mom. Runt preferred being alone. Her eyes flickered to the lights as the elevator descended. Rubbing her itching left palm against her leg, she was good at two other things besides computer programming; running and hiding. It was time to disappear again, only this time it would have to be permanent.

Chapter 9

Addie shivered in the darkness. The two men had brought her down to a level she didn't even know existed. The one she now recognized as Weston, had bound her hands in front of her with a sharp warning that if she resisted, he'd shoot her.

He had then proceeded to push her into the back of a van. She caught a brief glimpse of Merrick being loaded into a second van before the doors closed. Biting her lip, she blinked back the tears that threatened to fall. She should have listened to Merrick. She shouldn't have come into work tonight.

Guilt filled her at the selfish thought. No, it wouldn't have been right to not have tried to help him. Still, his haunting words filled her with dread – Weston killed the guard – Crawford was dead and couldn't help him now. What she didn't understand was how they knew she was aware of what was going on? Surely Crawford wouldn't have told them after he warned her to keep her mouth shut?

Pushing her hair out of her eyes, she leaned her head back against the metal side of the van. It had started to move slowly several minutes earlier. She had no idea where they were taking her or what they would do.

"Please, I don't want to die," she whispered in the darkness.

* * *

The next four hours blurred together in a mixture of exhaustion, terror, and worry. The van she was in arrived at another location. She was pulled from the back and shoved toward the back of a semi truck trailer. Turning her head, she saw an immaculately dressed woman in a tan pantsuit studying her with a cold look of disappointment.

"You think that he will want her?" The woman was saying to Weston.

"Markham seemed to think so," Weston replied. "If not, he'll kill her like he did the last bitch."

Addie paled at Weston's answer. Merrick had killed a woman? Addie felt sick that she had been about to help him escape before she remembered his promise not to hurt her. Still, what if he was lying.

Hell, it wasn't like he would have said 'Yeah, release me and I'll kill you before I leave to return to my world.'

Maybe the woman had been trying to hurt him. Still, she wasn't about to find out the hard way, if she could help it. She gulped in a deep breath as her eyes flashed toward the open doorway leading outside.

Panic gripped her in its steely embrace when the guard pushed her forward again. She started to turn away from where Weston, the woman, and Merrick were, but the guard behind her stepped in the way and forced her back around. Twisting the opposite direction, she pulled her knee up and struck the man in the stomach. The moment he bent over, she brought her tied hands down across the back of his head.

She didn't bother looking behind her. Instead, she sprinted for the opened door. She only made it five steps before she stumbled and fell to her knees when she felt the stinging burn cut along her upper arm. Tears burned her eyes as she knelt on the floor with her head down.

A cry of pain burst from her lips when a thick hand pulled on her ponytail. She tried to grab the hand wound in her hair even as she rose unsteadily to her feet. The man holding her jerked her around and struck her hard across the right side of her face. It took everything inside Addie to lock her knees so that she wouldn't sink back to the floor again.

"I warned you, if you tried anything I'd kill you," Weston growled, pulling Addie's head back so that she was forced to stare into his eyes.

"Wait!" The woman said when she heard an unearthly howl of rage. She turned to look at where the alien male was fighting savagely against the chains holding him. His eyes were glued to the blonde's face. "Don't kill her."

"We don't need this," Weston retorted.

"You don't, but I do," Rockman replied in a calm, serious voice. "Put her in the cage with him in the back of the trailer."

Addie whimpered when the man holding her pulled her across the warehouse floor. She wanted to struggle, but something told her if she did, it would be for the last time. Instead, she stumbled beside him. It took a moment for her to realize what they were going to do.

"Please... no," she cried out in a husky voice.

She fell forward several steps as Weston released his grip on her hair and placed his hand between her shoulder blades and pushed her toward the cage. Her hands wrapped around the bars to keep from falling. Pure, undiluted terror poured through her when she saw Merrick's face.

His eyes were glowing a dark silver with black flames in the center of them. His face was a mask of rage and his teeth… His teeth had lowered like they had the night before, only this time, she was seeing them up close and personal.

Merrick, she whimpered in fear. *Please don't kill me.*

"Oh my," Rockman whispered, studying the caged creature as if seeing him for the first time. "I have to have more time."

"It won't happen, Doc," Weston muttered, staring in fascinated horror at the savage beast chained to the thick plate of steel that made up the back wall of the cage. "He is too fucking dangerous and he has made some pretty fucking powerful friends here."

"Who?" Rockman asked, turning to stare at Weston. "Why do you think he has made any friends here on Earth?"

"Because Cosmos Raines is looking for him," Markham stated, stepping out of the shadows. "I've just received word that Keiser has been shut down. Raines has his security going through the building with a fine tooth comb."

"Raines…," Rockman repeated. "He's just a billionaire playboy."

"He's more than that," Markham replied in a steely voice. "I've given you a new plaything to work with. I know what your plans are, Doctor Rockman. You better hope it works. You have four days to get your clone or they are both dead."

Rockman raised an eyebrow at Markham before she smiled. Bowing her head in acknowledgement, she glanced at Weston's stony face before turning to run her eyes over the back of Addie. It would appear at least one of the men weren't as stupid as she thought.

"Put her in the cage with him," Rockman ordered. "If she is still alive when we get to Reno, I'll get my specimen one way or the other."

Addie cried out and struggled as the door to the cage with Merrick in it was opened. With a hard shove, she screamed when she was pushed roughly forward. Strong arms closed around her body in a crushing grip and her face was pressed against heated skin.

She could feel the vibration in the metal of the cage as the door was slammed shut behind her. Fierce shivers of shock began rocking her body despite the heat surrounding her. Another whimper escaped her when the cage was lifted by a large forklift and slid into the back of the semi-trailer. A moment later, she was sealed in darkness as the doors to the trailer were closed and locked.

Addie, a soft voice pierced through her terror-filled mind. *Hush, now.*

"Please... Please don't k... kill me," Addie whispered into the darkness before a dim light came on to cast an eerie glow in their long, narrow prison. "I was going to help you. Please don't kil.... kill me."

* * *

Merrick rested his chin on the top of Addie's head. It had taken almost an hour to get her to stop shaking. He wanted to check over her injuries, especially where he could see the blood on her arm. The problem was, every time he started to relax his hold on her, she would try to jerk away from him. So far, the only thing she had allowed him to help her with was breaking the plastic binding around her wrists.

Closing his eyes, he ran his fingers along her cheek. After twenty minutes of holding her, she had begun to wilt in his arms. He had carefully lowered them both down to the cold floor of the metal box. It took him another ten minutes of holding her tightly on his lap away from the cold before she finally relaxed against his chest.

I will keep you safe, Addie, he murmured over and over. *I will do anything to keep you safe.*

"You won't... hurt me like that man said you did the other woman?" She asked in a small, tentative whisper.

"Never," he promised. *Never, my bond mate.*

"I told you not to call me that," she reminded him before releasing a tired sigh. *I'm so tired.*

Sleep. I will watch over you, Merrick pushed soothingly.

I'm sorry I didn't help you get free, Addie thought back. *I... Oh!*

Relax, Addie, Merrick whispered when he felt her pulling away.

"No, you have to let me go," she replied excitedly. "I forgot! I have my cell phone! In my bra!"

"You have a communication device?" He asked startled.

He felt Addie nod. A wave of regret pulled at him when she reluctantly moved away from his warmth. Reaching up, he watched when she felt around inside her bra. A shaft of need burned through him when he felt the heat in her cheeks when he slid his fingers inside her blouse next to hers.

"Stop that!" She said furiously, smacking at his hand. "I can get it out by myself."

"Where is the fun in that?" Merrick chuckled.

Addie's head came up so fast at his teasing that it collided with his chin. They both muttered a silent curse, he in his language and she in hers, at the contact. For some reason, that seemed to be the straw that broke the camel's back. Her eyes widened briefly as she gazed up at him.

A surprised giggle escaped her at the unexpected teasing. The giggle turned to a soft gasp when he suddenly groaned. His right hand rose to tangle in her hair while his left gripped her side to prevent her from moving away from him.

"Merrick," Addie whispered in uncertainty.

"Yes, my Addie," he replied, slowly pulling her closer to him.

"I'm not..." Her voice died as his lips closed over hers.

Strange emotions rose up and crashed over him as he held her still. He tilted his head and coaxed her to open for him. He had seen part of a vidcom of J'kar's mate, Tink, doing this to him. Since then, he couldn't get the thought of what it would feel like out of his mind.

To have a female respond, on her own, without the use of the chemical from a male's bite, would be unheard of. Prime females needed the chemical her male released into her blood to become sexually aroused. Without the chemical, her body would not release the pheromones needed for reproduction.

Life had been lonely for him and the other males of their clan. The females of mating age in his clan had all been claimed. Most of his people seldom left the Eastern Mountains except when it was time to participate in the shrinking mating ceremony. Those that returned without a mate faced a lonely existence.

Merrick started when he felt the tentative touch of Addie's tongue against his. Opening further for her, a low groan of need echoed as he followed her slow dance. The feeling of being one, whole, for the first time in his life set a wave of need through him. This is what it meant to have someone of his own.

Her hand slid over his shoulder to tangle in his hair. Her lips moved more frantically against his and she turned until she was facing him. Her other hand started to move up his chest before she pulled back with a sharp cry of pain.

"Addie." A curse escaped him that he had forgotten to check her injuries. "Show me where you are hurt." *Let me look at your injuries.*

Addie bit her lip, refusing to look back up at him. *My arm is what hurts the most,* she admitted.

Merrick didn't reply. He scooted her off his lap so he could see her right arm better. Taking it carefully in his hand, he pushed the thin jacket off her shoulder. She was wearing a short sleeved dark blue shirt. He pushed up the sleeve far enough to see the damage.

A red mark, about an eighth of an inch wide and almost half an inch long ran across her upper forearm. It had stopped bleeding, but looked painful. Bending, he ripped a portion of his shirt from the bottom of it. He was gentle as he carefully wrapped it around her arm.

"I will kill him," he muttered under his breath.

He turned in surprise when Addie touched his chin. A frown darkened his brow when she looked at him in frustration. She touched his lips, then pointed to her eyes before tapping her forehead.

"You have to look at me when you speak. Or, you must think what you are saying to me, for me to understand you," she said in a husky voice.

"Why?" Merrick asked in a puzzled voice.

"I can't understand what you are saying otherwise," she explained. "I need to see how your mouth shapes the words or when you talk to me in my head to know when you are trying to ask or tell me something."

"This is not the case for all humans. Cosmos often had his back to me or others when he was communicating with them," he commented.

"He is not deaf, I am," Addie replied, studying his lips.

"Deaf?" Merrick replied in shock.

Addie nodded. "I lost my hearing after an illness when I was sixteen," she explained. "I have to tell you, hearing you in my head after being alone for so long is a little freaky."

It took a moment for him to understand what the word 'freaky' meant. She seemed to understand his confusion because she used the index finger of her left hand to make a series of circles at her temple, crossed her eyes, and stuck her tongue out. A low chuckle escaped him until he saw her wince and touch her cheek.

I will kill him for hurting you, he said, brushing her fingers aside so he could look closer at the bruise forming.

You can't kill people, she replied before going very quiet. *Is it true... that you killed a woman?*

Merrick's fingers paused against her cheek. He hated the uncertainty and slight tremble of fear that flashed in her eyes. Releasing a sigh, he shook his head.

No, I did not kill her, but Weston did, Merrick said. *Doctor Rockman wished for me to mate with her.*

"Mate! As in have...." A deep blush rose in her cheeks.

He nodded grimly. "I refused," he stated.

"Oh! Why?" She asked.

Merrick grunted and sat back against the bars. His eyebrow rose at her question before he sought the words to explain. His eyes followed her as she gingerly pulled her jacket back over her wounded arm.

"I did not find the female attractive," he stated bluntly. "She smelled."

Another blush rose over Addie's cheeks as she watched his mouth while hearing his words in her head. At first he thought of just speaking to her silently, but he liked that she watched him. Knowing that she could not hear, answered several of the questions he had last night.

Her surprise when she turned to see him even though he had made noise and her silence when he waited for her to speak now made sense. The fact that she was not a part of Doctor Rockman, Weston, or Markham's group was a relief. He felt a moment of regret for the guard who had tried to help him. Before he left this world, he would keep his promise to help Crawford's mate.

"I didn't mean that!" Addie muttered in a low voice. "I meant why would they say you killed her when you didn't?"

Merrick's eyes lit up in amusement. "I might have frightened her... a little," he admitted.

"What do you mean by 'a little'?" She asked in suspicion.

"The female lost consciousness when I wrapped my hands around her neck," he reluctantly confessed.

"I rendered her unconscious. When Weston ordered the guard to remove her, I did not expect him to kill her."

"Oh God," Addie whispered, wrapping her arms around her waist. She jerked when she felt the bump from her cell phone. "Damn it! I have a way to save us and I'm such a dope, I keep forgetting! I swear I'm too stupid to live sometimes."

"Never!" Merrick interjected. "You should not say such things."

Addie glanced up and rolled her eyes before focusing on the phone again. She needed to know who to call. Shaking her head, she glanced back at Merrick.

"You said you knew how to contact your friends to come help you," she murmured in a husky voice. "What is their number?"

Merrick looked at Addie's pale cheeks and strained expression. Regret burned through him that she was in such danger. Rising from where he was sitting, he moved to sit next to her.

"Cosmos said to call this series of numbers and someone would come," Merrick replied.

He watched as Addie carefully punched in the numbers he had memorized. She bit her lip and held the device up. He rose, helping her to her feet, and watched as she walked around the small cage. It took a moment before she turned back to look at him. Tears of frustration burned in her eyes as she stared at him in dismay.

"There is no signal," she whispered.

Chapter 10

Merrick's head jerked up several hours later when he felt the transport slowing down. He didn't wake Addie. She had fallen into an uneasy sleep a little over an hour before, and he could feel her exhaustion.

A low rumble of warning escaped him when the doors to the back of the trailer opened several minutes later. His arms tightened instinctively around Addie when she stirred. He hugged her closer to his body when he saw Weston.

"Looks like Markham was right again," Weston commented with a raised eyebrow.

"Yes, he was, wasn't he?" Rockman replied with a satisfied smile. "Have them delivered to the lab."

"Yes, ma'am," one of the guards responded.

* * *

"Merrick?" Addie whispered in a husky voice as she blinked sleepily up at him. "Where are we?"

I am not sure, he replied. *They will be moving us. I will not let them take you away from me, Addie.*

Addie struggled to sit up as his words sunk into her tired brain. She rubbed her eyes, ignoring the fact that she was still sitting on his lap. Fear began building inside her when she saw the forklift heading toward them.

"The phone," she whispered, turning to look up into his eyes. "We have to try to call again."

Merrick shook his head. *Not yet. There is not enough time.*

"Okay," Addie replied, turning toward him so she could slide the phone back into her bra.

Merrick's lips twitched when she looked up and caught him staring down the gap in the front. Her silent snort echoed through his mind as she adjusted her shirt. Lifting his hand to her chin, he tilted her head back so that she was looking into his eyes.

"I will protect you," he promised.

* * *

Addie tilted her head to the side and studied him. A sad smile curved her lips. She knew that he meant what he was saying. She could 'feel' it to the depths of her soul. But, she was also aware that some things were out of his control. Keeping her safe was just one of them.

"We'll get out of this," she replied, shivering when the cage jerked and rose slightly off the floor of the trailer. "I don't know how, but we'll get out of this."

She leaned into his hand when he cupped her cheek before pulling back and rising to her feet. He rose up and steadied her when she almost fell as the cage was lifted from the back of the semi-trailer. She reached out and gripped the bars to keep from falling.

Several men were shouting to each other while Weston and Dr. Rockman watched them. Merrick moved to stand protectively behind her, gripping the bars on each side of her.

I'm not totally helpless, you know, Addie informed him. *I'm the youngest of six kids, three of which were boys. Zach, Colin, and Brian all showed me some really good moves in case I ever needed them.*

You will not! I will protect you, Merrick stated, eyeing the movement and position of each person.

And if you can't? Addie pointed out. *I'm not saying you won't try. I'm just saying, if push comes to shove, I can help. The first chance I can get to call, I will.*

I told you…, Merrick started to say before he jerked as two long red darts struck him in the shoulder.

Addie's eyes widened when she saw him reach up and jerked them out with his left hand. His face had contorted again into a mask of rage. Her arms instinctively reached out as he swayed and started to fall to one knee.

Addie! Merrick's slurred voice echoed through her.

I'll protect you, Merrick, she whispered as she helped guide him to the floor of the cage. *I won't leave you alone again.*

Addie ran her hand over his cheek as his eyes fluttered shut. Whatever they had shot into him had to be an incredibly powerful drug to knock him out so quickly. She glanced up when she felt the cage bang against the floor. Fury drove her to her feet when Weston and Dr. Rockman walked toward it.

Addie didn't stop to think, she just reacted. Signing as fast as she could, her voice rose in fury. For once she didn't care if she was speaking in a loud voice.

"Why are you doing this to him? What do you want with him? With me? Why? Why would you treat others like this? Don't you care that it is wrong? Don't you have any morals? Any ethics? Any sense of humanity?" She yelled.

"My, my," Dr. Rockman chuckled, looking over Addie's bruised, furious face. "Who would have known our alien friend would prefer a furious Pollyanna, to a real woman?"

"Fuck you," Addie replied, glaring at the woman. "You don't know what a real woman is! If you did, you would never behave like this!"

"It looks like your kitten has claws, Doc," Weston laughed. "You'd better be careful."

Rockman's eyes narrowed on Addie's face. This time, a sneer pulled at her lip and she looked Addie's curvier figure over with a wave of distaste. She didn't give a rat's ass about claws. She could always remove them, one at a time, if necessary.

"Get him into his new home. Bring the girl to the lab," Rockman said, turning away. "I need to see if she is ovulating."

Addie frantically glanced around when Weston opened the door to the metal cage and several men came inside. There was nothing she could use as a weapon to keep them back. She rushed toward one man when he bent to grab Merrick by his ankle. Pushing him back, she yelled as loud as she could.

A scream of frustration burst from her when the man and two others grabbed for her. Kicking and screaming, she fought as hard as she could to break free. One of the men roughly jerked her arms behind her back while the others held her squirming body down.

She cried out in pain when two of the men lifted her up. The one man had his hand around where the bullet had grazed her. Throwing her head to the side, she headbutted the guy. Unfortunately, it was on the side that was already bruised and just made her hurt even more.

"I will walk, damn you!" She cried in frustration. "Let me go."

The moment the men released her back on her feet, she turned and kicked him in the shin. The man yelled and jumped out of range of her when she glared at him again. Straightening her shoulders, she tried to toss her hair out of her face.

She froze when she felt a hand brush the stubborn strands away from her face. Addie couldn't resist snapping her teeth at Weston's fingers when they got close to her mouth. The sharp tap on her bruised cheek caused her to quickly pull back.

Glaring up at him, she waited for him to speak. Indecision flooded her when he continued to stand in front of her, staring down at her. That feeling turned to terror when he suddenly wrapped his hand around the back of her neck and pulled her forward.

For a split second, Addie didn't know what to do when Weston's lips came down over hers in a crushing kiss. She pressed her lips tightly together, refusing to part them even when he tried to force her. Just when she thought he was finished, he bit her bottom lip. Still, she refused to open for him.

Finally, he pulled away and released his grip on her. Stepping back, he stared at her with a look of appraisal, as if he couldn't quite make up his mind about her. A slow, unnerving smile curled the corner of his lips.

"Perhaps if the Doctor doesn't want you, I might," Weston said.

Addie shook her head fiercely from side to side. Weston just chuckled and nodded his head to the two guards silently standing on each side of her. She jerked her arm away when one of the men reached to touch her. Glancing back over her shoulder, she saw four other men lifting Merrick's unconscious body onto a gurney similar to what the hospitals used to move patients around.

She pushed down the fear threatening to choke her and instead focused on where they were taking her. One way or another, she was going to escape. She didn't know how, but she wasn't going to just roll over and die.

No, I didn't give up when I was sick and I'm not going to give up now, she thought fiercely as she followed the guard in front of her through the brightly lit corridor.

Chapter 11

"What have you found?" Cosmos asked, leaning back in his chair.

"The body of the guard," Avery replied. "The hard drives for the security system are gone. We located where they were holding your alien friend."

"How did they get past RITA's surveillance of the area?" Cosmos demanded, looking at the multiple screens in front of him.

"There was an underground maintenance tunnel. It looks like they may have used it. RITA is checking the cameras in the area where they would have gone above ground," Avery answered.

"I've got some footage, Cosmos, " RITA piped in.

Cosmos looked over the grainy images of two vans pulling away from an underground parking garage almost four blocks from Keiser. They were identical. He tapped on the screen, enlarging the back of the second van.

"What else do you have?" He asked in a gruff voice.

"We've found another guard. I will be interrogating him after Trudy gets done doing an analysis. It looks like he has some of the dead guard's blood on him," Avery commented. "I'll let you know the minute I find out anything."

Cosmos looked over his shoulder when he heard a low rumble of disapproval. His eyes softened for a moment when they flashed to his wife, Terra, who was watching him with concerned eyes. It was almost four in the morning. The rumble sounded again, forcing his eyes back to the small group of Prime warriors standing behind him with their arms crossed. He grimaced when he saw the tight mask of disapproval on the face of one of the men.

Core Ta'Duran was Merrick's first cousin. He had been a royal pain in Cosmos' ass ever since Merrick disappeared almost four and a half months before. Correction, he had been a pain in his ass ever since he met Avery.

He didn't know, or want to know, what his head of security had done to get the huge guy's attention. He was afraid it might be another case of a Prime warrior finding his bond mate. Avery hadn't mentioned anything to him yet. Whatever was going on between the two, he hoped it didn't cause any more diplomatic issues than he was already having to deal with.

On top of dealing with Core's demands, he was working on his promise to Teriff, the Leader of the Prime. He had sworn that he would do everything in his power to find Merrick. It would appear the Prime council threatened to take a more active role if he wasn't found soon.

Cosmos had promised his new father-in-law that he would inform him immediately of any new information in an effort to help him keep the council happy. Between Core, Teriff, and Merrick, Cosmos was about ready to wash his hands of the lot of them! A deep sigh escaped him when he felt Terra's hands on his stiff shoulders.

"You know you don't mean that," she whispered in his ear. "You need rest. You've been working too much again."

"It is getting harder and harder to keep both your father and the President from sending in forces. That will only get Merrick killed. We know he is alive. My team just needs a few more days," Cosmos said, leaning his head back against her chest. "Once this is over, I want the two of us to go somewhere."

"Mak has an island off the coast," Terra murmured. "We can go there and be alone. Well, almost alone."

"You are amazing, you know that, don't you?" Cosmos chuckled, tilting his head to kiss her.

"Do you think you can focus on something other than my daughter?" Teriff demanded, coming to stand next to Cosmos.

"Father," Terra murmured in reproach.

Teriff flushed, but remained stubborn. "I wish to finish this. Every time your mother has made plans for the evening lately, something has prevented me from being there. Tilly has been showing her how to use the restraints. I want to see what she has learned," Teriff complained.

Cosmos covered his groan with a cough and turned back to the monitor. "That is way too much information, Teriff," he muttered under his breath.

"Why? Perhaps Tilly should show you as well," Teriff suggested. "I am sure she would be receptive to teaching you as well."

Cosmos couldn't keep the chuckle from escaping. "The last thing I need is instruction from Tink's mom," he assured Teriff. "I think I have a pretty good idea of some of the things she'll share with you."

"Why?" Teriff asked again. "Have you used them with Terra?"

That was too much for Cosmos. His sex life with Terra was not something he was about to discuss with her father. He scowled darkly at his father-in-law. He wanted everyone out of his lab, out of his warehouse, off of Earth, and out of his life!

Except for you, Terra, Cosmos whispered silently.

Terra's husky laughter filled him with warmth. *I know what you meant, my mate,* she replied, glancing over to where a shimmering door suddenly appeared next to Core. *I think you are about to get your wish.*

"What the fuck! Core, no!" Cosmos growled, turning to look over at where Terra was staring. "RITA!"

Cosmos glared at where a series of coordinates were displayed across the top of the monitors along with blueprints to the building. Aggravation poured through him and his fingers curled as he watched the three warriors disappear through the portal. He should have figured out a way to dismantle the damn things.

"Please tell me they are just going to return to their world," Cosmos asked in a grim voice. "Please tell me you did NOT give them Avery's location."

"Of course they are returning to their world," RITA said. "You know they can't move from Point A on Earth to Point B on Earth without causing some major temporal damage."

Cosmos ran his hands over his face and looked up at the ceiling in an effort not to pull the plug on one of the best inventions he, and Tink and Tilly Bell, had ever invented. Still, for just a moment it might not be such a bad idea.

"Cosmos," RITA replied in a soothing voice. "Core is worried about Avery."

"I know, RITA. I know," Cosmos replied, releasing his breath and sighing as a slender pair of arms wound around his waist. Turning, he pulled Terra into his arms and just held her for several long minutes before he spoke again. "It's just that it's very dangerous to have so many aliens running around all over the place. Avery can handle this."

"I don't think it is Avery that RITA is worried about, Cosmos," Terra said, leaning back so she could cup his face between her palms. "It is very difficult, even painful, for a Prime warrior to be separated from his bond mate. Avery has been avoiding Core and he can no longer allow that. He needs her, not just physically, but mentally."

Cosmos' hands moved down over Terra's slender form. He could understand what she was saying. The longer they were together, the more difficult it was for him to be separated from Terra. That was one reason why he didn't personally go on any more missions. The knowledge that if something happened to him, that Terra would be in danger of wasting away, was too much for him.

Sighing again, he released Terra and turned back to the monitors. "RITA, play the video of the vans back again and see if you can track where they went."

"I'm on it, Cosmos," RITA replied, cheerfully.

Chapter 12

Merrick groaned as he came awake. Memories flooded his mind and he rolled unsteadily to his feet. He frantically reached for Addie.

Addie! Addie! Where are you? Answer me! Merrick demanded.

He stumbled to the metal door of the cell he had been placed in. It was very similar to the one they had him in back at Keiser before they moved him to the cage. Pounding his fist against the metal framed door, he tried to clear his vision so he could see through the narrow window.

Addie!

I'm okay, Addie's shaky voice replied. *I think... I think they are bringing me down to you. Doctor Rockman told them to return me to your cell.*

Merrick didn't reply. He bowed his head and rested his arms against the door as he drew deep, calming breaths. He felt like his mind was splintering. The last few months of captivity, combined with the constant drugs and tests were bad enough, but to know that he had a mate that he could not protect was almost too much for the fragile strand he held on to.

His head jerked up when he heard the sound of footsteps coming down the long corridor. Relief swelled through him when he saw Addie's curvy figure. Her hands were bound in front of her and she looked very pale and tired.

"Get back," one of the guards demanded. "We've got orders to kill the girl if you try anything."

A low snarl escaped Merrick, but he stepped away from the door. The men only opened it far enough to push Addie through. The moment she was clear of the door, he crossed back to grab her, twisting to put his body between her and the guards.

"Doc says if you behave, the girl lives," the guard stated.

Merrick kept his back to the men, refusing to acknowledge them. His arms held Addie's trembling body close to his. He finally heard the men joking as they walked away. Only when the sound of their voices faded, did he release Addie. Leading her over to the long single bed against the far wall, he gently turned her so she could sit down.

He knelt in front of her and tenderly cupped her chin. A dark frown creased his brow as he studied the bruise on her cheek, another on her forehead, before he touched her lip which also had a small dark discoloration.

"Tell me what happened," he demanded in a low voice. "Did they hurt you?"

Addie studied his lips even as she heard his words in her mind. She shook her head, touching her cheek, then forehead. A small wince escaped her when she licked her bottom lip.

"My cheek was already bruised from where Weston hit me earlier. I got a new one when I head-butted one of the guards. He grabbed my arm and it hurt," Addie said with a crooked grin. "I kicked him in the shin too."

"What happened to your lip?" Merrick asked, tenderly rubbing the dark spot.

Addie rolled her eyes. "Weston kissed me. I guess he didn't like that I didn't respond. The guy is an asshole," she muttered. "He's nothing but a big bully. He wanted to intimidate me, I think."

Merrick closed off his mind, not wanting Addie to hear his murderous thoughts. Weston would be the first one he killed. Markham second if he was here, if not, he would hunt him down after he killed every other human that had held him captive.

"What did Doctor Rockman do to you?" Merrick forced out over the sick feeling in his stomach. "Did she… hurt you?"

"No," Addie replied with a puzzled frown. "Except for asking me a bunch of questions and taking a blood sample, she was actually pretty reserved. I was just glad when they put the plastic ties on me again, they put them in the front instead of the back."

Can you try your communication device again? Merrick asked.

It won't work. There is still no signal. I think it is because of all the metal. I only had a brief moment to check it when I used the bathroom outside of Doctor Rockman's office, Addie replied with a sigh, glancing around and wondering if there were any cameras or listening devices in the room.

I will look to see if there are any, Merrick replied, brushing Addie's hair back from her face. *I am sorry you are in harm's way, Addie.*

You aren't the one who did it, the others are, she reminded him with a crooked grin. *But, since you're feeling so guilty about it, I'll let you figure out how to get us out of this in one piece, okay?*

It took Merrick a moment to understand that she was teasing him. A low, rusty laugh escaped him and he shook his head in wonder. Yet again, Addie was proving to be a surprise.

"You are a beautiful mate," Merrick murmured, stroking her bruised lip with his thumb.

Another smile tugged at his lips when she rolled her eyes and looked at him in disapproval. He could hear her automatic denial, just as he knew she could hear the determination in his 'voice'. She shook her head, pulling away from his caress and glanced around the room. He knew she was trying to avoid looking at him.

"What do you think is going to happen to us?" She asked in a suddenly husky voice.

"I will try to protect you, but…." Merrick paused as he thought about what happened back in the cage when they arrived. As much as he wanted to promise her again that he would protect her, he was defenseless against their drugs. He turned his head away from her. "I will do everything I can to protect you, Addie. I wish I could promise you more."

He turned his head back when he felt Addie's fingers against his chin. She touched his lips, then the corner of his eye, before she laid her hand softly against his cheek. It was a gentle reminder that she needed him to look at her when he spoke. He had shut her out part of the way through his sentence.

"But...?" She asked.

"I do not know if I will be able to," he admitted.

Then, we'll have to figure out a way together. I have my cell phone. I'll try again the first chance I get. Oh, and I took a set of keys from the guard back at Keiser. If they try to lock you up with the same locks, we can use that, she whispered into his mind.

Sit here while I check the room, Merrick ordered, rising to his feet.

* * *

Addie watched as Merrick explored every inch of the small room they were locked in. She scooted back until her back was against the wall and pulled her legs up. The room was cold, but that wasn't what was causing the goose bumps on her arms.

She might be in danger, but she wasn't dead. The man roaming the room was totally hot, even if he was an alien. His long, black hair hung down well past his shoulders.

Correction, massive, muscular, delicious shoulders, she thought, making sure she had a firm wall around her thoughts.

A sigh of relief escaped her when he didn't stop what he was doing to glare at her. She felt pretty sure her thoughts were confined within her own head. Feeling more confident, she let her eyes roam over the rest of him.

He was tall, but nothing that would be too unusual for a human. He had to be at least six foot five, maybe a little taller. Hell, two of her older brothers were almost that tall. The difference between her brothers and Merrick wasn't in height, as much as, in build. Neither Zach, Colin, or Brian had muscles like that, no matter how much they worked out.

Addie's eyes lit up when he bent over. She couldn't help, but admire the way the loose fitting pants he was wearing suddenly grew taut over his ass. A blush rose in her cheeks when he straightened and turned. She glanced away, pretending to be studying the door.

After several seconds, her eyes moved back to him. His eyes were a dark silver with black pupils that appeared to shimmer in the center. His nose was a touch broader, but if anything, it made him even sexier. Overall, it would be hard to tell from a distance that he wasn't human. The biggest difference was his muscular build, his eyes, and the fact that his teeth did that weird up and down thing.

Okay, so even that was sort of hot in a horror movie kind of way, she thought, glancing at him under her eyelashes.

"Are you a Vampire?" She asked suddenly, wincing when she bit her lip again. "I mean, you look like one when your teeth do that thing…" Her voice faded when he turned to gaze down at her. "I'm just wondering."

"What is a Vampire?" Merrick asked.

"They are a... Well, they're dead and they suck people's blood and...," her voice faded when she saw the amused look on his face. "I don't know. They're Vampires."

"I do not drink blood," he replied, walking to where she was sitting with her knees drawn up.

"Oh," she whispered when he sat on the edge of the bed. "It was just that your teeth... they kind-of, you know, they..." Addie opened her mouth and wiggled her fingers in a downward motion.

"It is natural," he chuckled. "A warrior's teeth elongate during battle and during..." His voice faded and his eyes lit with amusement and something that looked a little like mischief.

"During what?" Addie signed as she spoke.

"Mating," he replied with a grin, capturing her hands as they fluttered in front of her. "What is this you do with your hands? It is very beautiful."

Addie's cheeks flushed when he lifted first one, then the other to his lips. She tried to pull them free, but he tightened his grip on them, refusing to let her go. Her breath caught in her throat as he leaned into her.

"It is the way I speak to others who can't hear. Merrick, I don't think this is such a good idea," she whispered, straightening her legs when he tugged her forward.

"I think it is a very good idea, Addie," he whispered, lowering his head and pressing his lips against hers.

For a moment, everything faded away. They were no longer in a cell, in a strange place. He wasn't an alien male. There was just the two of them.

Addie responded tentatively to Merrick's gentle kiss. It was different from the first one he had given her. That one had been hot and intense. This one was more exploratory, as if he knew he needed to go slow. He released her hands and tangled his fingers in her hair, deepening the kiss when she opened to him.

For a brief second, doubt started to cloud her mind, but she pushed it away. Life was about the adventures, both good and bad, that you encountered in it. Sometimes the two crossed paths at the most unexpected times.

Addie let her fingers explore the contour of Merrick's chest. A shiver of need flashed through her at the hard muscle under the thin shirt he wore. Her fingers skimmed over them to his shoulders.

She didn't protest when he suddenly turned her until she was lying on the narrow bed. The vague thought that danger made people react in unexpected ways they normally wouldn't, swept briefly through her mind, but she pushed it right back into the little box it popped out of. She was enjoying this too much to quit just yet.

Her arms wound around his neck as he covered her body with his. A shaft of unexpected need pierced her. It was so sudden that it made her gasp.

"Addie," Merrick whispered, pulling back to look down at her with blazing silver eyes. "I need you."

The flames were back in them. This time instead of being frightened by it, she was curious. Sliding her right hand up to his cheek, she rubbed her thumb against his high cheekbone.

"I...," she whispered. "I don't understand this. I've never felt this way before. This is crazy."

* * *

Merrick could hear the confusion in her thoughts and her rationalization of why she was reacting the way she was. He wanted to deny every reason she was coming up with, but something told him it was important for her to accept that they were going to be together on her own. Well, he would give her as much time as he could. Once they were free, all restrictions were off. He would take her back to the Eastern Mountains and she would be his forever.

"You are tired," he said, noting the dark circles under her eyes. "Rest for now."

"Thank you, Merrick," she whispered, knowing deep down that he could sense her confusion.

Merrick bent and pressed a brief, hard kiss to her lips before he pulled back again and rolled onto his side. He wrapped his arms around Addie when she rolled onto her side to give him more room and pulled her back against him. A smile curved his lips when she snuggled back against him, before it died on his lips as he looked around the small area.

Except for a toilet, sink, and the bed, it was devoid of anything else. He pressed a tender kiss to the top of Addie's head as she relaxed. Her soft teasing words echoed in his mind.

You aren't the one who did it, the others are. But, since you're feeling so guilty about it, I'll let you figure out how to get us out of this in one piece, okay?

There has to be a way to either escape or use the communications device Addie had to contact Cosmos' people. Now more than ever, he had a reason to fight back. He just needed to do it without putting Addie in any more danger than what she already was, he thought in frustration.

A sense of peace settled over him when Addie unconsciously moved her hand to curl around his. Even though he knew she did it in her sleep, it gave him hope that she would accept her fate as his mate. Forcing his body to relax, he slipped into a light sleep, visions of him and Addie back among his people giving him hope and comfort.

Chapter 13

Avery looked at the guard who was sitting back in his chair. The desire to wipe the smug expression off his face was beginning to become unbearable. She itched to see him sweat.

She had already interrogated the other guard who had been at the gate. It was clear he hadn't known what the hell was going on. In fact, he had been concerned about another employee called Addie Banks, who did Housekeeping. So far, the team had found the dead body of the guard whose girlfriend had called them and no one else.

"Listen, asswipe," Avery said with a cold glare. "I don't have time for this. I want to know where your friends went."

"I know my rights. I haven't done anything wrong," Josh Johnson said. "I want an attorney."

"If you haven't done anything wrong, then, you don't need an attorney," Avery commented. "Though, I think finding a dead body might be considered a touch unlawful."

"I didn't kill Crawford," Josh replied with a shrug. "I didn't know anything about it until you mentioned it a few minutes ago."

Avery knew the bastard was lying through his teeth. She started to turn away to tell Trudy and Rose to leave the room, she didn't want them to see what she was about to do, when the familiar lights of a portal suddenly appeared in the room. She heard

Trudy and Rose's low curses at the same time as she heard Johnson's louder one.

"What the fuck?!" Josh muttered hoarsely, pulling the chair that he was handcuffed to up with him when he twisted and watched in horror as three huge warriors stepped through the shimmering door. "What the hell is going on?"

"That, Mr. I-didn't-do-anything," Avery replied sarcastically, "is something you are going to wish you really hadn't seen."

Avery watched warily as Core Ta'Duran stepped through the portal. The last thing she needed right now was another damn headache in the form of a huge ass, bossy, in-her-face, alien. She had plans for him, but she refused to become distracted before she had completed her current assignment.

"What are you doing here?" Avery demanded, folding her arms across her chest and looking at the three men with a raised eyebrow. "Does Cosmos know?"

"I do not answer to Cosmos," Core snapped, glancing at the handcuffed male. "Have you found Merrick?"

"He was here," Avery replied in a clipped voice.

"But no longer?" Core stated more than asked.

"But no longer," Avery agreed, glancing to where Josh Johnson stood pressed as far as he could go into the corner with the chair attached to him. "I was about to have a conversation with Mr. Johnson here about that."

* * *

Core's eyes narrowed on the pale male. His eyes swept over him in distaste. He was beginning to intensely dislike the majority of human males. In fact, except for Cosmos, he would just as soon not have anything to do with another damn one.

"Why?" He asked bluntly.

"We found the body of another guard," Avery explained in exaggeration. "This one has the guard's blood on his shoes."

"What the fuck!" Johnson exclaimed, looking down at his shoes and turning even paler than he had been before. He had forgotten to check them after he dumped Crawford's body in the Biohazard waste container out back. "Listen, I was just doing what I was told. I didn't kill Crawford. I had to do it, if I didn't Wes... If I hadn't, I would have been next."

"Leave," Core ordered, not looking at Avery as he took a step closer to the trembling guard.

He heard the door open and close behind him. The human male knew where Merrick was and he would get the information out of him one way or the other. He was finished with wasting time. This had dragged out far longer than it should have.

"Core," Teriff's voice cautioned from behind him.

Core glanced over his shoulder at Teriff, before turning his head when he noticed that while the other two females had departed, Avery had not. She stood near the door, silently watching him.

"You should leave," he ordered.

"Since you shouldn't be here in the first place, I think that is a moot point," Avery reflected.

"I will get the information that I need, Avery," Core cautioned her. "All of it."

"What's he saying?" Johnson demanded, looking back and forth between Avery and the creature that had stepped out of the nowhere.

Core watched Avery's face turn to a blank mask as she turned to look at the guard. His respect, and curiosity, about her continued to grow. While she had maintained her distance from him, refusing to allow him close enough to touch her, he was certain she was his bond mate. The physical pull to be near her, have her, was becoming almost impossible to resist.

"He says you are screwed," Avery replied in a voice devoid of emotion. "If I were you," she continued, turning to look at where Johnson stood, "I'd tell him every damn thing you know."

"And... And if I don't?" Johnson asked hoarsely.

Avery shrugged her shoulders. "That's entirely up to you," she said, leaning back against the door. "Sometimes it can take a very, very long time to die."

Core watched as the male melted in front of him into a quivering mass on the floor. His loud sobs and pleas would not save him. He would not kill the man in front of Avery, though. Turning, he nodded when Teriff released a sharp command that would not translate in the device that each member of Cosmos' response team wore. With a nod, he stepped forward, snapping the arms of the chair. Grabbing the male by the back of his neck, he pushed him toward the portal that Teriff had opened.

"You can't take him yet! I need the information he has first," Avery demanded, straightening and glaring at Core.

"I will get the information," Core replied, nodding to Derik, who stood silently next to his father, to take the human. "What we do is not something a female should see."

"He is my prisoner," Avery retorted in a low, angry voice. "This is my assignment. We are too close to have it jeopardized now."

"I will get you your information," Core repeated, watching Avery's face closely as he continued. "Once Merrick has been returned to my world, you and I will finish this, Avery. You will not avoid me any longer."

Avery's delicate eyebrow rose and her mouth turned up at the corner. He had expected shock, perhaps denial, not the look of challenge she was giving him. A sense of forewarning shivered through him. This woman was not like Borj's mate, Hannah. This one was a predator, much like him.

"I never complicate a mission with distractions," Avery replied in a low, steady voice. "But, I do enjoy my distractions, big guy. When this is over, you'd better make sure you look over your shoulder, because I plan on taking you up on your invitation."

A curse escaped Core as Avery pulled open the door and disappeared through it. Forcing the confrontation to the back of his mind, he turned and disappeared through the portal. The sooner this mission was over, the sooner he could start one of his own.

* * *

Addie was startled awake when Merrick suddenly twisted and covered her body with his own. A low, menacing growl rumbled through his chest. She watched in fascination as his top teeth slid down. Instead of being afraid, she found it comforting to know that if she had to be in a situation like this, it was better to be in it with someone who wasn't human.

Turning her head, she looked at where he was staring. A frown darkened her brow when all she saw was the closed door. Sliding her hands up between them, she carefully touched his chin.

"What is it?" She asked in a husky voice.

Footsteps. I hear at least six different sets, he replied.

Addie opened her mouth to ask him how he could tell how many, but her mouth snapped closed when she saw the door open. Fear threatened to choke her when she saw Doctor Rockman's face among the group. The look of satisfaction in the woman's hazel eyes was enough to cause Addie's stomach to turn in disgust.

"We can do this one of two ways," Doctor Rockman said. "I can have the guards tranquilize you again and take Addie, or you can cooperate with me. If you try anything, the guards have been instructed to kill her. Do you understand?"

The dark snarl that escaped Merrick had the guards aiming for him. Terrified that they would shoot him again, she cupped his face between her hands and pulled it down until he was forced to look at her. She frantically shook her head back and forth, a look of pleading in her eyes, before she spoke in a low, trembling voice.

"Please," she begged. "Do as she says."

I will not let her hurt you, Merrick snarled with such force that Addie winced from the fury in his thoughts.

If she thinks you'll cooperate with me here, it will give us a better chance of getting out of this alive. She'll think you are behaving and not be suspicious of me. We can use this to our advantage if she thinks it is a way to control you, Addie insisted. *If they knock you out, there is no way we can get out of here.*

Merrick bowed his head until his forehead touched hers for just a moment. Addie could feel him trying to get control of his emotions. She could also feel the fatigue pulling at him. It was only going on the second day for her and she was already mentally and physically exhausted and stressed to the point that all she wanted to do was curl up and cry, she didn't know how he had been able to endure it for months!

Please, Merrick. I really think if I can get a signal, we can get help, Addie begged.

She watched him pull back and close his eyes. After several deep breaths, he opened his eyes and nodded. A tentative smile curved her lips as he carefully shifted his weight off her and stood up next to the bed.

He kept his body between the men and Doctor Rockman and her. Addie tiredly sat up and swung her legs over the side of the bed. Pushing her hair out of her face, she stared at Doctor Rockman's satisfied face. For the first time in her life, Addie seriously considered using physical violence against another woman. She would love to snatch the bitch by the hair and drug her ass to see how she liked it!

"That was a smart decision," Doctor Rockman said.

"What do you want?" Merrick demanded.

Addie could see the surprise on Rockman's face at Merrick's sudden demand. The woman's eyes flashed back and forth between him and Addie before she looked back at him. A calculating look came into her eyes that immediately had Addie suspicious that the woman was up to something.

"The guards will restrain you and you will be escorted to the lab for additional testing. This will be the first time that I can perform some tests without you being under the influence of drugs. As long as you do the tests that I need, you and Addie, isn't it," Rockman asked, looking at where Addie was sitting on the bed, trying to follow along. Addie nodded her head. "Addie will be given time to refresh herself and return here. If you attack any of the guards, try to escape, or refuse to complete any of the tests, I will order her immediately terminated, do you understand?"

Addie could feel the rage in Merrick and laid her hand on the back of his thigh in an effort to remind him to remain calm. They needed to play along until they could escape or were rescued. No matter how bad it got, as long as they were alive, they had a chance.

Merrick, please, Addie begged silently.

I will do what she demands... for now, Merrick replied before closing off his thoughts.

Addie turned her eyes to the woman again as Merrick nodded his head. Rising to her feet, she bit her lip when Merrick stood stoically while two of the guards put shackles around his waist, wrists, and ankles. The sight of such a proud, powerful man reduced to this made her want to cry. There was just something so very wrong about chaining a creature so powerful.

"Take him to the lab," Doctor Rockman ordered. "I'll be there shortly."

"Yes, ma'am," one of the guards said. "Move it."

Addie's eyes remained focused on Merrick's back until they turned the corner at the far end of the corridor and she couldn't see him any longer. She jerked in surprise when she felt cold fingers touch her arm. Turning, she watched with wide, wary eyes as Rockman indicated for her to follow her.

Nodding, Addie's hand went to her stomach as it turned. She didn't know what was about to happen. It took everything in her to not touch the cell phone that she had hidden in her bra just to make sure it was still there.

Addie followed Doctor Rockman while the remaining guard followed. She was surprised when they turned the same corner and stepped into an elevator. The silence that had been such a huge part of her life since she was sixteen suddenly felt overwhelming.

I am here, Addie, Merrick suddenly whispered through her mind. *I will not leave you.*

Sorry for being such a wuss, Addie thought back as she watched the elevator numbers going up. *I swear, I don't know how you've kept your sanity. Two days and I'm ready for a straight jacket and a padded room.*

Who said I kept my sanity? Merrick teased back.

Addie bowed her head to keep the sudden grin on her face hidden. She hadn't expected his teasing, but it was definitely welcomed, she thought as warmth filled her. Who would have thought… an alien with a sense of humor.

Thank you, Merrick, Addie whispered. *Are you alright? Where are you?*

I am fine. Rockman wishes to see my endurance, Merrick replied dryly. *They have me on a machine and wish for me to run. They are not the brightest of scientists.*

Addie cleared her throat, trying to cover her choked laugh as a cough. She glanced over at Doctor Rockman who was studying her with a frown. Touching her throat, she emitted two short coughs with an apologetic smile.

I'll be alright now. If I get a chance, I'll try calling the number. Rockman is actually taking me up higher. I've got to go, Addie added. *Be safe and don't let them knock you out.*

I will behave, Addie, Merrick grumbled dryly. *Be safe yourself, my mate.*

I'm not... Addie rolled her eyes when she felt Merrick pull away with a chuckle. *Toad.*

She sighed as she followed Rockman out of the elevator and down yet another corridor. This section looked more like an apartment, than a lab. Glancing around, Addie felt a sense of hope surge through her. She could see the lights of buildings out of the seventh story window. They were in a city!

Where there's a city, there is bound to be cell phone reception, she thought with excitement. *Oh, Merrick, we may make it out of this yet.*

Chapter 14

Margaret Rockman nodded to the guard to stand outside of her new office as she stepped through the door. Out of all of the labs she had been given to use over the past four months, this one was the nicest. Markham had outdone himself this time, she reluctantly admitted.

Waving her hand to a chair, she stepped around the desk and sank down in the chair. Her eyes ran over the figure of the woman in front of her. Addie Banks was a bit of a surprise. From her early exam, she was five foot five inches tall, weighted in at one hundred, thirty-five pounds, twenty-two years of age, and was deaf due to an illness when she was in her teens.

Margaret decided Addie's thick blonde hair, green eyes, and curvy figure were the major attraction. Personally, she didn't give a damn. She just wanted something that she could study indefinitely.

"Addie, can you understand what I am saying?" Margaret asked with a raised eyebrow.

She watched as Addie nodded, signing as she did. "As long as you speak slowly and look at me, I can usually figure out what you are trying to say," Addie admitted in a husky voice. "Why are you doing this? Why did you take me?"

"Do you have any idea what a find such as this is to the scientific world? The fact that an alien life exists is beyond comprehension. I would have been insane to pass up a chance to study a live specimen," Margaret replied.

"You hurt him. How is that helpful? You... They killed the guard! You don't kill people in the name of science," Addie argued.

"How did you know that the guard had been killed?" Margaret asked with a raised eyebrow.

Addie shrugged and sat back in the chair she had sat down in. "The man who caught me said something," she replied, looking Rockman in the eye. "Why did you take me? I wouldn't have known anything. I just clean offices."

"But, you did know something, Addie," Margaret replied in a quiet voice. "Markham reviews the security tapes daily. He informed Weston of the transgression."

Addie paled and folded her hands together. "I didn't tell anyone about what I saw. I thought it was one of those experiments they do with college students needing extra spending money," she explained in a trembling voice. "Some kids from my classes were talking about doing it recently."

Margaret leaned forward and folded her hands carefully on the desk in front of her. She needed Addie's cooperation. So far, any sperm she had tried to retrieve from the alien had died shortly after she took it. Addie was at her peak chance for a pregnancy, according to the blood tests. She was young, and except for her hearing loss, healthy. The bonus was that the male appeared to find her attractive.

Not only that, Margaret was running out of time. She had three days until Markham returned to destroy her prized lab rat. Yes, time was running out and she had been given the perfect replacement. Margaret was a firm believer that things happened for a reason, and Addie had been at the wrong place at the right time, as far as she was concerned.

"Then, you can consider yourself part of this experiment," Margaret stated, watching Addie's face crease with a frown.

"What kind of experiment?" Addie asked.

"I want you to have intercourse with him," Margaret replied.

"What?!" Addie replied in disbelief, sitting forward and staring at Margaret as if she must have translated what she was saying wrong. Shaking her head, she concentrated on Margaret's mouth. "You want me to what?"

"I want you to have sex with him," Margaret repeated slowly. "It is the one... test I have been unable to study."

"NO!" Addie whispered in horror, rising out of her seat. "No, that is just... wrong! I can't... You can't... That is just... wrong on so many different levels!"

Margaret rose out of her chair as well, looking at Addie through narrowed eyes. Her mouth tightened at the look of horror on the young woman's face. Perhaps she had misjudged the situation and there was not a measure of attraction between her and the male. It wouldn't matter, she had no choice. It was Addie or nothing.

"Are you really so naïve, Ms. Banks?" Margaret asked in a cold voice. "Sex between species has been studied throughout history. I need to have a sample of his semen and you, Addie, will get it for me."

"No!" Addie said, shaking her head back and forth.

"Then, you are no longer useful," Margaret replied. "And neither is the male. I've done all the tests I need from him."

* * *

Addie watched in horror as Margaret picked up the phone on her desk and pressed a button. Panic struck her as she read the woman's lips. 'Kill him." Leaning forward, she grabbed Rockman's arm.

"No, no, I will do it," Addie said, desperately. "I'll do it."

"Cancel the order," Margaret finally ordered after several long seconds. "Get him cleaned up."

Addie pulled away as if she had been burnt. Fear, panic, and horror mixed together in a boiling acid that washed through her in torrential waves. She didn't know what to do.

She had never had a physical relationship. She had spent all of her time and energy trying to learn how to live all over again, sex and relationships, had been moved completely off the burner! Now, it was not only moved back on, it was turned on high. How the hell was she supposed to seduce a guy like Merrick when she…

Oh shit, she thought. *What if he is built all weird?*

Addie? What has happened? I can feel your panic, but you have your thoughts shielded, Merrick's deep voice pushed ruthlessly through the wall she had constructed.

I'm okay. How about you? She asked, her mind churning with confusion.

They are moving me, Merrick replied in a cautious voice.

I'm still with Rockman, Addie said faintly. *I have to focus on what she is saying. I... I'll see you soon.*

Addie, Merrick whispered.

Yes?

You are an amazing female, he said in a gruff voice before pulling away from her.

You have no idea, Addie whispered as she focused on what Rockman wanted.

* * *

Ten minutes later, Addie watched as the door to the bathroom closed behind her. The pile of clothes in her arms felt like weights instead of silk. Rockman had handed the delicate dress that was more suited for a cocktail party than a prison to her, with the instructions she had thirty minutes to make herself desirable, or she and Merrick would be terminated.

"Nothing like the threat of death to put somebody in the mood," Addie grunted out as she dropped the pile on the floor next to the sink.

Reaching into her shirt, she pulled her cell phone out of her bra. Pressing the button, she waited for it to turn on. Tribulation gripped her in its greedy grasp as she waited to see if she had a signal. She almost cried in relief when she saw four bars appear at the top of the lighted display.

Her fingers trembled uncontrollably as she pressed her finger to the button. Glancing at the door, she bit her lip and hurried over to the shower. Turning it on, she leaned back against the wall and tapped the phone icon.

Addie pressed the number at the top of her recent list and waited for the phone to vibrate to let her know when it was connected. It took both of her hands to hold it. The moment the connection showed, she typed quickly.

"Please help us," she tapped out, glancing up at the door. "We are being held prisoner."

"Where are you?" The returned message replied. "Is Merrick with you?"

"Yes. I don't know. We didn't see where they were taking us," Addie typed. "They have threatened to kill us. They have already killed one person."

"Can you describe where you are?"

Addie growled in frustration. Raising the phone in front of her, she spoke in a low voice. It was frustrating not being able to see and hear the phone.

"I'm deaf, so I can't hear you," Addie whispered, keeping her eyes glued to the door. "I worked at Keise Institute in Housekeeping. Last night, a... man named Merrick and I were taken by force. He gave me this number to call. Please, I don't have much time. We are in a basement section of a building. They had… have us locked in a cell. I will leave my cell phone on as long as I can. I have to go."

Addie pulled the cell phone away and glanced at it. Excitement burst through her when she saw the message. Tears blurred her vision, but she pushed them away.

Grabbing the towel off the towel holder, she hid her phone under it. She quickly stripped off her dirty clothes and stepped under the hot water. She washed quickly, her mind playing the message over and over.

Help is on the way, sweetheart. You are in Reno, Nevada. Stay strong, you'll be free soon.

Merrick? Addie called, reaching for him as she lathered her hair.

I am here.

Help is on the way, Addie whispered in excitement. *We'll be free soon.*

They have taken me back to my cell, something strange is going on, Merrick replied in a voice filled with tension.

Why do you think that? Addie asked, swallowing nervously.

Rockman did not come to the lab and the testing was cut short before they returned me, he replied.

Yes, well, I think I'm going to be returned soon, Addie responded.

What did she do to you? He asked.

Just talked to me, Addie replied. *Merrick…*

Yes?

I… Never mind. I'll be there soon, Addie said with a sigh. *Just concentrate on the fact you'll be free soon.*

We will be free soon, Addie.

We'll be free soon, she replied.

Addie quickly finished her shower, dried off, and dressed. She grimaced as she bent and turned her head down so she could dry her hair. Something told her a wet head was not sexy.

She quickly ran the brush through it after it was semi-dry to contain the fluffiness. Ignoring the makeup, she glanced in the mirror. Her eyes suddenly seemed way too big for her face. The hot shower, combined with practically standing on her head to dry her hair, had put a rosy glow on her cheeks making makeup unnecessary.

The dark blue dress hugged her figure, making her self-conscious. She never wore clothes this tight. She looked with distaste at the matching high heels. The whole outfit screamed 'call girl'.

Breathing deeply, she gripped the cell phone in her hand, glancing once more at the message on the screen before she reluctantly turned it off and slipped it into the pocket of her jeans. There was no way she could hide it in her bra. It was too delicate and the dress too tight for the bump of a cell phone to be concealed. Addie really hoped that they didn't take her clothes away from her.

She quickly collected the pile and turned when the door to the bathroom opened. The pleased look in Rockman's eyes made her stomach turn again. Once again, Addie couldn't help but wish she was a more violent person.

"You clean up very nicely," Rockman said with a nod of approval. "Remember what I said. If you don't get the sample I want, I will terminate both of you."

"You aren't… You aren't going to wat… watch us, are you?" Addie asked in a low, husky voice. "I can't… I can't if, you know… I won't do it, if anyone is watching."

Addie hated the trembling in her voice. There was no way she could make love with Merrick if she knew they had an audience. Her face flooded with heat when she thought of him and her doing…

Rockman's chuckle pulled her out of her reverie. Resentment flashed through her. Her first time should have been a special time with someone that she loved! Not because this, this horrible, evil woman wanted to complete another test.

"I won't do it," Addie snapped in fury. "You can kill me now if you think I'll let you watch us like some kind of pervert."

"Don't tempt me," Rockman replied in a voice as hard as steel. "You'll seduce our alien friend and get the specimens I need or I will let you watch me dissect him before I kill you. I don't have time for your sudden modesty, Ms. Banks. You will do what you are told. I know Weston is interested in you. Perhaps you'd like to warm up with him first?"

"No! No," Addie replied in a trembling voice. "It is just… this will be my first time."

"Your first…." If Addie thought the woman would be sympathetic or understanding to the fact that she was a virgin, it disappeared at the woman's delighted laughter. "This is too good to be true. Well, my little virgin, you get to seduce the big, bad alien. Perhaps he can sense your innocence, which is what is turning him on."

"You are a horrible person," Addie hissed, clutching her clothes to her chest. "I hope you get what you deserve!"

"I hope so, too, my dear Addie. I really hope so," Rockman chuckled. "The guard will escort you back. Make sure you do a good job."

"Go to hell," Addie muttered, walking past Rockman with her head held high.

* * *

Addie breathed in deep, calming breaths on the journey back down to the lower levels. The one thing keeping her going was knowing that they would soon be rescued. Her face heated when she thought of what was about to happen. Glancing at the guard's face, she knew there would be no help from him.

I can do this. I know I can do this, she kept whispering to herself.

What can you do? Merrick's voice asked just as the guard opened the door pushed her inside.

She would have fallen if not for Merrick standing, waiting for her. Panic erupted inside her until she glanced up into his eyes. They were burning with the dark flames again.

"I... Rockman," Addie swallowed. "Rockman wants me... She wants me to... Wants us to... Oh God."

Addie bent her head, unable to look at Merrick. How did she tell him they were supposed to make love? Hell, how was she supposed to do it when she couldn't even tell him? She didn't have a clue how far their rescuers were from them, but she really hoped they came in the next five minutes.

She raised her eyes to him again when he gently tilted her chin back. Moisture pooled in them as she stared up at him. Confusion, uncertainty, and a sense of panic gripped her in its tight fists.

"What does Rockman want?" He asked in a gentle voice.

Addie bit her lip, wincing when she caught the tender spot between her teeth. Drawing in a deep breath, she stepped back and set her clothes down so he could see her. She knew that while she was uncomfortable in the dress that Rockman had given her, Merrick was not immune to it if the stunned expression on his face was anything to go by.

"She wants me to seduce you," Addie admitted in a soft voice. "She says if I don't that she will kill you, then me."

"Addie," Merrick's hissed voice echoed in her mind.

"I told her I wouldn't do it, but she said if I didn't," Addie paused and drew in a shaking breath. "She said if I didn't that she would dissect you in front of me. I honestly think she would do it, Merrick. I honestly think she is crazy enough to cut you up in the name of 'science'."

She closed her eyes when he stepped forward and cupped her cheek in his large palm. Her breathing increased when he slid his other hand around her waist and pulled her close. Her eyelashes fluttered open when he drew her close again.

"Look at me," he whispered, rubbing his thumb along her bruised cheek.

"I've never done this before, Merrick," she admitted. "I always thought my first time would be special."

For a brief second, Merrick remained frozen. Even his thumb had stilled on her chin. It was as if he wasn't quite sure of what she meant at first. Addie knew the exact second the translation connected with his stunned brain. A fury of color rose in her cheeks when his muttered curse exploded through her brain.

Chapter 15

Merrick had been suspicious earlier when the 'tests' had been cut short. He had been wary from the very beginning. It was true that most of the time, he was barely able to function. They had to keep him drugged up, to keep him under control. The few times he had managed to work the drugs out of his system was when he had been able to kill a guard or two.

This time, not only had they not kept him partially sedated, the tests had been mundane. He had been chained to a device and told to run. After less than twenty minutes, the guards had removed him and taken him to a facility to shower. That was another first. Normally, he was restricted to whatever cleaning he could do with a damp cloth and the sink in his prison cell.

He couldn't imagine Rockman ordering him to bathe just so she could kill him. He had been in the middle of his shower when he had felt Addie's jubilation. Relief and hope soared inside him when she told him that she had been able to call for help.

He had thought the trembling in her voice had been from that. Now, he realized it was for a much different reason. When he heard the slight clicking of heels on the tile before she arrived, he had first thought it was Dr. Rockman returning. It wasn't until the door was opened and he saw Addie's golden hair and beautiful green eyes that he knew it was her.

When the guard pushed her through the door, he had automatically reached for her. It wasn't until she stepped back that he realized that she had also bathed and changed.

Addie's softly spoken words 'Rockman wants me to seduce you' had shocked him, but nothing prepared him for her next statement. Desire, the need to protect, and the primitive urge to claim all slammed into him at once. The loneliness he had felt, combined with the stress, melted away as he captured her lips.

His fingers tangled in her long, blonde hair, holding her still as he continued to ravage her lips. A moment of regret surged through him when she winced, but even that dissolved when she started kissing him back. A long moan escaped them both when he slid his other hand down over her ass.

"Addie," he groaned. Tilting her head back, he looked down at her. "I will make this special for you. I promise."

He slid his trembling fingers down over her cheek before leaning down and tenderly brushing his lips across the bruised flesh there. He knew one way to help her through this. The chemical in his bite would heighten her pleasure and make her more receptive to him. From the little he had learned from RITA2, this was not something that a human male did for his female.

The chemical was necessary for Prime females. It helped their body become more responsive and heightened their enjoyment. Without it, their bodies did not produce the necessary lubrication needed to accept the male. At least, that was what he had been told by his father and the other elders of his clan when he was growing up. He was not entirely sure how a human female became ready for a male, he could only hope that the chemical he released into her helped.

Addie, I am sorry, Merrick whispered even as he felt his teeth elongate.

Sorry for what? Addie asked before a loud gasp and startled cry escaped her.

Ecstasy and relief washed through Merrick as he sank his teeth into the curve of Addie's neck. A shiver escaped him and his arm tightened around her when she started to struggle. Instead of releasing her, he held her still, gently running his tongue against the skin of her neck while the chemical his body produced released into her.

He knew the moment she began to feel it. Her skin flushed and her hands began kneading his back. The scent of her fear was quickly replaced with that of her arousal. Focusing, he withdrew his teeth from her flesh and ran his tongue over the two, small wounds.

He may have lied slightly when he said he didn't drink blood. While he didn't in the way she was referring to, he did enjoy the coppery taste of her blood as he sealed his mark on her. A groan escaped him when Addie turned her face into his neck and pressed a hot, wet kiss to his skin.

The groan dissolved into a low growl when she nipped his flesh. Knowing that she was an innocent was the only thing keeping him from taking her up against the wall. If she continued running her hands all over him, he just might forget that.

"Addie," he warned as her hands slipped lower to grab his ass.

"I want you, Merrick," Addie murmured as she continued to press hot kisses to his neck. One of her hands slid around in between them. "You feel so good."

Merrick choked back another curse when he felt her hand run over the front of him. All information that he had learned from the time he was old enough to discover how to please a female, vanished when she slid her hand down the front of his pants and wrapped her fingers around him.

"Addie," he groaned again, pushing against her soft palm.

He pulled back far enough to grip the neckline of her dress. He hoped that she didn't plan on keeping it. With a quick jerk, the material parted between his hands. Pushing the silky cloth off her shoulders, he muttered a curse when she released his cock and pulled her hand out of his pants.

That curse died when she shrugged off the ruined remains of the dress and grasped the front of his pants at the waistband. He gaped down at her when she slowly gripped both sides and pulled them down. In his dreams, he had imagined a female like this being his mate, but in reality, he had thought it would always be a fantasy… until now.

Merrick's eyes closed partially as Addie ran her hands up his legs. The warmth of her breath caressed his skin, making him clench his teeth as his cock responded. He remembered a vidcom that the first traitorous human male had shown him. It was one about...

"Blood of the Goddess," Merrick's hoarse cry exploded in the room when Addie's lips brushed the tip of his straining cock. His fingers tangled in her hair and he held her still while he willed himself to remain in control. *Addie, you have to stop.*

I... don't want to, she replied, looking up at him. *If something should happen, either before or after your friends come...*

Do not think that, he growled, glaring down at her.

I want to know, just in case. I want to feel alive, Addie continued. *I want... you.*

Merrick pushed away the feeling of guilt. He didn't know if it was Addie really speaking, a reaction to his bite, or a combination of his bite and the threat that Rockman had given to kill them. At this moment, he could understand her feelings about wanting to feel alive. After the months of constant pain, lack of sleep, and confinement, he thought he would never feel alive again. Now, gazing down at Addie as she looked up at him, he couldn't imagine a life without her.

"Addie," he choked out over the lump in his throat.

A soft, tender smile lit her face. Turning her attention back to her exploration, she leaned forward and pressed a kiss against his thigh. The shy look in her eyes before she turned her gaze down caused the lump in his throat to swell until he found it impossible to speak.

Bending, he grabbed her hands as they reached for his throbbing cock. He was too on edge to let her continue. Her pleasure would come first, even if it killed him. He had sworn that her first time with him would be special, and it would be.

Helping her to her feet, he kicked his pants to the side. Releasing her long enough to grab the bottom of his shirt, he ripped it over his head and tossed it aside. He swallowed hard when he got his first real look of Addie without the dress she had been wearing.

Her long blonde hair had fallen over one shoulder and laid across her right breast. She was wearing a dark blue lacy garment that cupped them, pushing the large mounds up until they practically overflowed. His eyes ran down over her curvy figure.

He liked that she was slightly plumper than the other human women he had seen so far. Dark blue lace covered her lower region, forming a teasing triangle that made him itch to uncover the treasure hidden beneath it. Reaching out, he touched the golden strands of her long hair. It was so different from the women of his clan. They all had black hair just as he did.

"I want you, Addie," he said, looking into her eyes.

Addie's eyes twinkled with mischief as her gaze ran down his body before returning to his face. A grin curved her lips and she tilted her head. The movement pulled the hair covering her breast away and he caught a hint of darker skin under the lace.

"I can tell," she replied. "Now, are you going to do something about it?"

Merrick chuckled and reached for her again. This time, he wrapped one arm around her back and the other under her knees. Picking her up, he turned and laid her down on the bed. For just a moment, a flash of resentment rushed through him again at the narrowness of it. It was a reminder of where they were.

Don't, Addie said, looking up at him when he laid her down before slipping her high heels off her feet and tossing them aside. *For just a little while, I want to forget where we are and what is happening. I just want it to be the two of us, no one else, just the two of us.*

Then, it will be just the two of us, Merrick promised. *If we were on my world, I would take you up to my home in the trees. There, I would spread you across my bed and take you until the mist settled among the mountains. We would be the only ones. We would lose ourselves in the cloak of the mountain as she sleeps.*

His eyes softened when he saw the tears shimmering in her eyes. The whisper of her thoughts caressed him. For a moment, she could see the Eastern Mountains that he loved so much in his memories. He embraced them, pulling them forward so that she would feel as if she was there with him.

Merrick continued to project the visions to her as he leaned down and brushed his lips across hers. When she opened for him, he deepened the kiss. His hands moved down, cupping her breasts in the lacy garment. With a flick of his fingers, he snapped the front clasp and released the lush mounds. A sense of satisfaction swept through him as he covered her body with his. Leaning on his left elbow so that he didn't crush her, he continued to kiss her while he used the fingers of his right hand to tweak her taut nipple.

"Merrick!" Addie gasped, turning her head and closing her eyes as he pinched her nipple this time. "Oh!"

Merrick shifted his weight, placing his knee between her legs to force her to open for him. Sliding down her body, he continued to press hot kisses to her exposed skin. His heated gaze locked with hers as he hovered over her distended nipple. In slow motion, he lowered his mouth until she could feel the heat of his breath against her skin.

He paused, waiting. The look of desperation in her eyes changed to determination when he continued to stare at her. He felt, more than saw, Addie's hands move to grasp each side of his face. With a slight tug, she pulled his mouth down over her breast. A low cry of pleasure escaped her when he sucked deeply on the pebbled tip.

"Yes!" She hissed. "Oh, yes!"

A low rumble, almost like a purr, escaped him when the fragrant scent of her arousal touched him.

Sucking deeply on first one, then the other nipple, he balanced his weight on his knees as he gripped the thin material covering her womanhood. Snapping the side, he tossed the ruined material to the floor when she lifted her hips.

Unable to resist, he remembered a portion of the vidcom that spoke of a male pleasuring a female with his tongue. The idea of tasting Addie's desire, of taking her, ignited the fire inside him that was quickly turning to molten lava. The feel of his cock, brushing against the covers as he leaned over Addie, just increased his sensitivity.

He wanted her, needed her, with a hunger that defied anything he had ever experienced before. This was more than just a chemical reaction, this was something deeper, more emotional than just a physical need for release. Being with her filled an emptiness inside him and calmed the constant edge of feeling that something was missing inside him.

Pressing his lips to the soft skin of her stomach, he glanced up to watch her face as he slid his fingers across her labia. The slick feel of her desire showed that she was just as affected by him as he was of her. He slowly pushed past the soft folds, enjoying the low groan that filled the air as his fingers sank into her liquid heat.

"Merrick," Addie cried hoarsely in a voice filled with laden desire and need, relaxing her thighs to encourage him to continue his exploration of her body.

Shifting his weight, he emitted a low snarl of frustration. He pulled his fingers from her body and slid off the bed at the end. Reaching down, he pulled her down toward the edge of it and kneeled. He grasped each delicate calf in the palm of his hand and draped her legs over his broad shoulders.

His eyes darkened to molten silver when he saw that this position opened her to him. His eyes flashed to hers. She gazed back at him, her arms over her head, clutching the top of the bed frame with her hands.

"Stay like that," he ordered, turned on by the thought of binding her wrists to his bed frame in his home. "Do not resist me, Addie. I am too close to losing control."

Her eyes widened in surprise, but she nodded her understanding. Merrick's eyes returned to the glistening thatch of curly blonde hair and sweet warmth. He glanced up when he felt Addie pull him closer with her legs. Touching the soft curls, he was rewarded when she bowed upward into his touch.

His fingers slid down along the slick folds and he carefully opened her to him. He had noticed every time he touched the small nub concealed within the soft folds, she would moan and jerk. Touching it again, he watched as her face flushed with pleasure and she rocked against his finger.

Bending forward, he suddenly captured the hidden gem with his tongue. He slid two fingers into her at the same time, pulling a low shuddering cry as he pushed forward. A low growl escaped him when her legs stiffened and her heels drove into his back when he began caressing the nub as he slid his fingers back and forth, going deeper with each movement.

He paused for a brief second when he felt a barrier prevent him from going deeper. In frustration, he nipped at the nub that he was teasing as he drove his fingers past it. Addie's loud cry echoed and she froze for a moment. He waited, concerned that he had hurt her somehow. After a moment, she relaxed and began rocking her hips.

Relief flooded Merrick and he pushed another finger into her as he teased the swelling nub. The next time Addie cried out, he knew he had brought her to pleasure as the warm ambrosia of her desire and blood flowed around his lips. Now, she was ready.

Merrick was trembling as he carefully slid her legs from over his shoulders. He rose on unsteady legs and gazed down at Addie. Her body was limp, her face flushed and her lips slightly parted. His gaze moved from where her eyelashes lay like crescents against her cheeks to where her breasts rose and fell as she drew in deep breaths. Stepping to the side of the bed, he carefully lifted her higher on it.

Her eyelashes fluttered opened and she stared up at him with dazed eyes. He gently settled her back against the lone pillow before he climbed over her body again. Her legs parted so he could slide between them. The movement opened her to his straining cock.

Wrap them around my hips, he ordered in a hoarse, strained voice.

Balancing himself on his elbows, he lowered himself over her. His body began to tremble uncontrollably when he felt the tip of his cock brush against the soft curls. Pushing slowly forward, he began to pant as her slick heat surrounded it.

"Now, now, I claim you as my mate," he said intensely, gazing down at her. "You are mine. For now and for always. There will never be another. I claim you as my bond mate. For always."

His left hand rose to tangle in her hair when she started to shake her head. Capturing her lips again, he surged forward, burying his cock as far as he could inside her. A shudder shook them both at his possessive claim.

Addie's soft channel greedily fisted him. The hot walls of her vagina stroked his length and he could feel every inch of her as he began moving back and forth. Intense emotion swept through him as he tangled his tongue with hers.

Breaking away, he gritted his teeth as he felt the pressure build to an unbearable level. His balls drew tight and hard as he continued to drive into her. Each slick push taking him deeper until he swore he could feel the tip of his cock touching her womb.

Merrick buried his face against her shoulder and tightened his arms around her until it was hard to tell where one began and the other ended. Opening his mouth, he felt his teeth descend again. The need to mark her, prepare her womb for his seed, drove him to the edge as the fear of losing something so precious, tangled with the primitive urge to mark her as his.

Biting down on her shoulder, he could actually feel the chemical in his sensitive canines releasing into her. Her body reacted to the added stimulation. A long, loud groan exploded from him when her legs tightened around his waist, her heels digging into his buttocks, as she shattered around his cock. The force of her orgasm snapped the last of his control and he exploded into her with a force that took his breath away.

Merrick withdrew his teeth from her tender flesh, clamping his lips over the wound while he pulsed deep inside her. His eyes closed and a low moan escaped him as another jet of his semen burst from him to wash her womb with his seed. Holding Addie tightly against his chest, he remained locked to her as the powerful orgasm held him in its greedy grasp.

Pressing a kiss to her shoulder before turning his head to press another one to her exposed neck, he breathed deeply as his body began to relax in contentment. A smile curved his lips when Addie wound her arms around his waist and held him. Pressing another kiss to her neck, he pulled back to gaze down at her.

You are now mine, he said, pressing his hips against her.

Has anyone ever told you that you have a one track mind? Addie teased.

Merrick started to respond to her teasing when the sounds of rapid footsteps approaching caught his attention. His head turned and a low, dangerous snarl escaped him. He pulled himself out of Addie and rolled to his feet. He sensed danger coming.

Get dressed, Merrick growled in a low, menacing voice. *We are about to have company.*

Merrick grabbed his pants and slid them on, standing between the door and Addie as she quickly slipped her jeans and shirt on, ignoring her undergarments. His gaze flickered to her communications device when it hit the floor when she grabbed her shirt. She quickly slid it into the front pocket of her jeans as the door suddenly opened.

He roared out when two men raised the familiar guns containing the potent darts filled with the drugs they use to knock him out. Two of the darts hit him in the chest, knocking him backwards.

"No!" Addie's loud cry echoed in his ears even as he felt the drugs began to take effect.

"Chain him to the bed," Dr. Rockman ordered. "Get the girl. I need to get her to the lab as soon as possible."

"Merrick," Addie cried out, reaching for him and pressing something cold and hard into his hand. *Keep this.*

"No!" Addie screamed, struggling when a guard gripped her from behind and pulled her away from where Merrick, half knelt, half lay against the bed. "Merrick!"

Addie, Merrick's slurred thoughts called her. *Don't...*

Chapter 16

Avery glanced down at the message on her phone late the next morning. Her eyes widened in surprise before a sense of satisfaction washed through her. She wouldn't need to wait for Core to retrieve the information she needed. It would appear that the missing Housekeeper, Addie Banks, had succeeded in outsmarting the bad guys.

"RITA, I need Intel on the location you were able to obtain from the cell phone signal," Avery ordered. "Get Trudy, Rose, and the Runt on it. I need Team Two ready to be briefed and ready to depart in fifteen minutes. Get me Cosmos."

"Information has already been sent. I have begun taking control over their computer system. All functions controlled there, including the security, and environment, should be completed within the hour. Team Two has already been alerted and are en route, as is Team One. Cosmos is online…. Now. Oh, and Runt has disappeared again," RITA said.

"Shit!" Avery muttered just as Cosmos came online.

"What do you have?" Cosmos asked, fumbling with the buttons on his shirt.

"RITA received a call on the secured line you set up for Tansy's mission. Addie Banks, an employee of Keiser Institute, connected to RITA's system and said that she and Merrick were being held prisoner. She didn't know where they had been taken, but she left her cell phone on long enough for RITA to lock into the signal. They are in Reno, Nevada at the Destiny-Brinks Industries building," Avery explained, heading out of the office and into the private elevator that would take her to the helicopter on the roof. "She said Doctor Rockman had threatened to have them killed."

"Do you believe her?" Cosmos asked, scanning the information on Addie Banks, as well as, a transcript of the conversation.

"Yes, she worked in Housekeeping. She just started a few weeks ago. The guard at the gate was very concerned about her. She is deaf and he feared that she might have been killed along with Crawford," Avery replied. "The caller used a TTY service for the hearing impaired, and warned RITA that she was deaf."

"What about Merrick?" Cosmos asked.

"She said he was alive. I have no reason to think she was lying," Avery answered.

"I've called in a favor," Cosmos said. "The President offered several members of the military's new elite squad on terrorism. They have been briefed by the President on the situation."

Avery grimaced, but kept her opinion to herself. She knew that the President was aware of their alien visitors. Tilly Bell had made sure of that when she, her three daughters, and five huge-ass Prime warriors suddenly appeared in his office. Granted, Tansy was there to warn the President that the Vice-President had made arrangements to have him assassinated, but that didn't mean they had to introduce him to

Cosmos' Gateway invention, *and* aliens from another star system to boot!

"You want to what?" Avery asked, pausing in dread and disbelief when she heard Cosmos next order.

"I want you and the Team Two to work with Teriff and Core. You'll use the Gateway to get inside. Team One will come in as a distraction. You have to get to Merrick and the girl before anything happens to them. RITA has a list of levels she has calculated to be the most likely where they will be held from the security cameras and blueprints of the building," he explained.

"That would mean we have to go to their world," Avery pointed out, hiding her dismay.

"It is too dangerous to go from one point on Earth to another. Avery, you have to find Merrick and get him out this time. Teriff understands what has been going on, but the Prime Council is ready to override his orders and send in their own rescue unit. The President has briefed me that this must be avoided at all cost."

Avery didn't say anything. There really was nothing to say, Cosmos was right. Hell, it wasn't that big a deal, and as Cosmos pointed out, the main priority was getting the two hostages out in one piece. It would also give them an edge those holding Merrick wouldn't expect.

"I need one of your portal devices," Avery replied.

"Core and Teriff will meet you on the roof. RITA has been in contact with RITA2, I still haven't figured out how the hell she does that," Cosmos muttered in a distracted voice. "She'll get the information to the Teams."

"I want one of those damn things, Cosmos," Avery snapped. "When this is over. Don't forget."

"I won't, Avery, but remember it will only be a loaner. I don't know how many of the damn things Brock and Lan have created for the Prime. I'll have to see if RITA2 can get me a number," Cosmos replied. "Good luck and don't get shot."

Avery snorted. "I never get shot. I'm the one doing the shooting," she reminded him. "Have RITA monitor the mission. I want to get your alien and take out the bastards who think they can jerk us around."

"Just finish this," Cosmos ordered before signing off.

Avery pushed the button on the elevator. Drawing in a deep breath, she glanced up at the numbers. All she needed to do was keep her head screwed on straight, complete the mission, then she could get the damn alien male that had been haunting her dreams at night out of her system.

One, two, three… as simple as that, she thought as the door slid open and she stepped out onto the roof of her Headquarters.

* * *

Addie stumbled when the guard jerked on her arm again when she tried to look over her shoulder. She could see several guards lifting Merrick's limp body and settling it on the bed. Turning back around, she wished she could hear what was going on. For the first time in years, she realized just how much she missed her ability to hear.

Tears of frustration and worry threatened to overwhelm her. The only comfort she had was knowing that they hadn't killed Merrick. They wouldn't have chained him to the bed otherwise. Still, she didn't understand why they had drugged him and taken her.

She stumbled to a stop when she saw Weston standing next to the elevator with an amused expression on his face. She flushed when his eyes ran over her shirt. It was obvious that she wasn't wearing a bra. Fighting the urge to cover herself, she glared back at him in defiance.

Straightening her shoulders, she pushed her hair behind her ear when he walked toward her. She shot a nervous glance at Dr. Rockman when she appeared to say something to him. Whatever he said in return must have been scary because Dr. Rockman's mouth snapped shut and she glared at the back of his head in angry silence.

Addie flinched when she felt Weston's strong fingers on her chin. Turning until she was staring into his eyes, she suddenly had a sinking feeling that she knew what he was going to say. Merrick had checked their cell earlier, but not after they had both been taken out of it. She could feel her face flaming as Weston ran an appreciative gaze over her figure again.

"You are very beautiful in blue," Weston commented with a sickening smile. "Especially blue lace. You are also sexy as hell when you are on your knees."

Addie reacted without thinking. Her right hand flew up and struck Weston across the cheek. She clenched her stinging palm, slowly bringing it back to her chest as she waited for his retaliation. She turned her head when his hand came up. It took a moment to realize that he was rubbing his own cheek with a thoughtful expression and not striking out at her.

"I like a woman with a fire in her," Weston chuckled when she turned back to gaze at him. "After the doctor gets her sample, I'll have to see if you are as good a fuck as it looked."

"Never," Addie whispered, swallowing the nausea churning in her stomach.

Weston's hand suddenly snapped out and wrapped around her nape. He jerked her forward, capturing her lips in a kiss filled with promise. His eyes were twinkling with amusement when he finally pulled back.

"It will be interesting to see how long you resist me," he whispered before releasing her. "Go get your alien sperm, Dr. Rockman. Just make sure she takes a shower when you are done."

Dread filled Addie as she finally understood Dr. Rockman's strange demand. Her hand fluttered to her stomach. Rockman wanted something that Merrick would never have willingly given her.

Addie numbly stepped into the elevator and turned to look at Weston's mocking face as the doors close. Sudden hatred, deep and poisonous, poured through her, causing her fingers to curl into tight fists. Closing her eyes, she prayed for a miracle.

Please, please let whoever I called come for us before Dr. Rockman gets what she wants from me, she thought.

Addie opened her eyes as the elevator stopped. This time, it was on one of the lower floors. She swayed when the doors opened and Rockman stepped out and turned to look at her with a raised eyebrow.

"Well, come on," Rockman snapped impatiently. "I need to examine you and take samples."

The cold, heartless words snapped the rage burning through Addie. With a low cry of fury, she erupted in rage. Jerking forward, she pushed Dr. Rockman hard enough to knock her down. Addie didn't stop. She took off running as fast as she could, her bare feet flying down the long narrow corridor.

She was half way down it when a bright light suddenly appeared in front of her. Not stopping, she twisted, swerving into an open door and slamming the door. It appeared to be a small office. Addie grabbed the chair by the door and slid it under the doorknob before sinking down along the wall next to it.

It wasn't much protection. The walls were only solid half way up. The other half was frosted glass. Addie glanced up when she saw several dark shadows pass by. A frown darkened her face when she saw several looked like they were wearing helmets.

Standing up on shaky legs, she peeked along the edge where a thin section of the glass was clear. Her heart was pounding when she saw the uniforms on the several of the men. Her eyes moved to a tall, elegant woman who was wearing a heavy vest and yelling. Addie couldn't tell what the woman was saying from the angle she was peering through.

What really caught her attention was the huge male walking slightly ahead of the woman. He looked like Merrick! Trembling, Addie pulled the chair away from the door and slowly opened it.

A low scream escaped her when the door was suddenly ripped from her hand. Twisting, she tried to turn back into the room, but a hand tangled in her hair and forced her down onto her knees. Addie frantically tried to grab the powerful hand, but whoever had her continued to push her face toward the floor.

"No!" Addie cried out, unaware of the shouts around her. "Let me go!"

Addie stilled when she felt hard metal pressed against the back of her head. Closing her eyes, she waited for the shattering pain of a bullet. Her only hope was that Merrick would survive.

"Merrick," she whispered.

A loud gasp escaped her when she was suddenly rolled onto her back. The gun that had been at the back of her head was now pressed against the center of her forehead and she found herself staring into familiar blazing silver eyes. She blinked several times, trying to clear the tears clouding her vision.

She stared at the man's mouth, but she didn't understand what he was saying. Her eyes flickered to the woman standing over his shoulder. A frown creased her brow as the woman's mouth moved.

"Help me," Addie whispered in a husky voice.

"Where is Merrick?" The woman demanded.

"Downstairs," Addie replied, focusing on the woman's mouth. "The guards drugged him. Please, help us."

The woman paused and turned her head to talk to the man. Addie almost cried in frustration when the man's eyes blazed with fury. Raising a trembling hand, she touched his wrist.

"Please, my name is Addie Banks. Are you the ones who I contacted?" She forced out, not releasing his gaze.

"Damn it, Core, release her! She is the missing woman from Keiser," the woman was saying.

"Yes, please, help Merrick. Dr. Rockman... She threatened to kill him. There is another man down there," Addie said desperately.

Addie breathed a sigh of relief when the man pulled back and rose. Sitting up, she watched as he stepped back toward the door and disappeared through it. She was so focused on him, that she jerked when the woman touched her shoulder.

"One of the men will stay with you," the woman explained, staring intently at Addie.

Addie nodded, rising when the woman stepped back to the door and called out to one of the human men in uniform. Rising on trembling legs, Addie's gaze followed the woman and alien male that resembled Merrick as they quickly moved down the corridor.

Her eyes paused on Dr. Rockman who lay on the floor, handcuffed. She swayed when she saw the guard who had been with them. From the blood pooled around his head, she knew he was dead. Darkness clouded the edge of her vision and she frantically gripped the edge of the door frame to keep from falling.

She shook her head when the policeman, or whoever he was, turned toward her. Pulling back into the office, she slid down the inside wall. Addie pulled her legs up to her chest and wrapped her arms around them to steady herself. She didn't even move when the officer closed the door. She didn't care about anything at that moment except shutting out the world around her. Closing her eyes, she allowed the tears to come. For the moment, she was done with the world.

Chapter 17

Karl Markham paused, listening for the sound of footsteps. He had just arrived at the complex when he saw the vans approaching. A low curse escaped him when he recognized that he had arrived too late.

His inside contact had informed him that their current position had been compromised. He should have had time to get in, take the alien, and get out. He wanted to add the bastard's head to his prize list. This male was a predator, a killer, like him. For the first time in his life, he felt like he had something that was a challenge.

He had planned to take the huge bastard back to the island that he owned and hunt him just as he hunted the big game in countries all over the world. While his benefactors wanted to poke and prod the creature and Rockman wanted to dissect him like a frog, he wanted to see just how good the bastard was when he was the prey. To him, there was nothing more thrilling than the hunt.

Now, all of his carefully laid plans were about to be ruined. Bitter disappointment threatened to make him reckless, something that he never was. Pulling back, he watched as Weston exited an emergency stairwell. The guard standing in the corridor saw him at the same time. Weston raised his gun, firing at the guard at the same time as the guard fired at him.

Dark blood stained Weston's shoulder. Markham raised his own gun, aiming for the back of the guard's exposed upper thigh. A bullet in the right spot would cut through the main artery, not killing the man immediately, but allowing him to bleed to death in a matter of minutes. Pulling the trigger, he watched as the guard dropped. Stepping up to the fallen man, he kicked the gun further down the hallway.

"What the fuck happened? I thought you had someone on the inside," Weston muttered, clutching his shoulder.

"Markham, help me!" Rockman cried out, twisting awkwardly in an effort to sit up. "We have to get out of here!"

"I'm afraid there is no we, Margaret," Markham replied, pointing his gun at her head and pulling the trigger.

"Shit! You could have let her patch me up before you shot her," Weston cursed.

"She was a liability," Markham replied. "How bad is it?"

"Clean shot," Weston hissed in pain. "We need to get the fuck out of here. I don't know how the hell they got into the building."

"I don't either, but I plan to find out. Where is the alien?" Markham asked, checking his gun.

"Knocked out downstairs," Weston replied. "I was in the security office when I noticed the feed was off. I shut it down and pulled the hard drives and destroyed them. I was on my way upstairs when I heard gunfire."

"Where is the woman?" Markham asked, nodding toward a door at the far end of the hallway.

"I don't know," Weston grunted in a voice filled with pain. "Rockman wanted to test her after the bitch had sex with your newest target."

"The alien had sex with the girl?" Markham asked with interest.

"Yeah, it was hot as hell," Weston admitted. "Fucking made me want to have a bit of fun with her."

Markham thoughts turned to the pretty blonde as he and Weston walked further down the hallway toward the back. Perhaps, there might still be a chance to salvage his plans. It would depend on what happened to the girl. He would have to make sure he knew where she was, once they made it out of the building.

There was an unrecorded exit not in any of the blueprints. He made sure that all the facilities he chose had similar undocumented exits. This building had been refurbished two years ago by one of his clients who was paranoid about being trapped after a kidnapping when he was younger that cost him one of his ears.

Opening the door, he stepped inside and turned, waiting for Weston. With a nod, he pressed the hidden panel and stepped inside the narrow lift. Pressing the button, he looked at Weston's pale face.

"Do you need a doctor?" He asked.

"No, you can stitch me up," Weston replied. "It isn't like you've never had to do it before."

"True," Markham replied with a shrug. "It is a good thing our mother insisted we learn."

Weston nodded in agreement. As much as he had hated their mother, she had made sure they learned how to take care of each other. It was probably the only thing that had kept them both alive when they were younger. They sure as hell hadn't survived because of her motherly love for them.

* * *

Addie jerked awake when the door next to her opened. She blinked in confusion, expecting to see the guard from earlier. Instead, it was a different man. Fear threatened to choke her until she saw the badge on his vest. He said something, but once again, she couldn't understand as he had his face turned away from her.

She brushed her hair away from her face and tentatively reached for Merrick. Disappointment and worry filled her when she felt the unfamiliar emptiness. Glancing up as another grim faced man in uniform stepped into the doorway, she nodded when he motioned for her to stand.

Rolling to the side, she used the chair she had moved earlier to help her get up. The man at the door asked her something, but it was too much for her foggy brain to decipher. Signing that she didn't understand him, she touched her ear and shook her head.

"I'm totally deaf," she explained in a husky voice. "You will have to speak slowly and look at me so I can understand you."

"Are you hurt?" The man asked.

Addie shook her head. "No," she responded. "Where is Merrick? Have you found him?"

The two men looked at each other for a moment before the one who had spoken to her gave her a brief nod. Addie wanted to scream in frustration when the man didn't continue. Touching his arm when he started to turn, she motioned with her hand.

"Is he okay?" She insisted.

"Yes, he has been taken to a secure location where he can be evaluated. We need to get you out of here," the man insisted.

Addie knew when he turned away that she would get no more out of him. Stepping out into the corridor, she glanced down to where Rockman had been lying. Shock and horror froze her limbs when she saw the woman lying on her side, a pool of blood around her head.

Turning to the guard who had spoken to her, her eyes flashed past him to the body of the guard that was supposed to keep her safe. He was lying on his back, staring blankly up at the ceiling. Another pool of blood, this time around his lower limbs stained the white tile.

A low cry of distress escaped Addie and she swayed. She knew this time that the dark edges crowding her vision wouldn't be denied. The guard standing slightly behind her must have realized it too. His arms reached out to grab her as her knees buckled and she slowly began to fall.

* * *

Core nodded to the two men assigned to the President's special task force that were across from him. Glancing briefly over his shoulder at Avery, his lips tightened when he saw that she stood at least two feet behind him with her weapon drawn. He had wanted her to remain behind, but Cosmos had sent a message through RITA2 that his security chief was in charge of the mission and would go.

He would have ignored the human if not for the fact that RITA2 had disabled the Gateway devices. Brock, the Prime engineer who had discovered Cosmos' portable devices, had been stunned to learn that RITA2 had rewritten the programming in it and locked them out with a stern warning, either they cooperated with Cosmos, or they lost the ability to use the portal. Core had to admit, while he understood that RITA2 was just an AI program, she reminded him a lot of the human women with her stubbornness and wicked sense of humor.

"Sorry, darling," RITA2 had chuckled when Brock tried to bypass her security systems. "All's fair in love and war, and Cosmos will always come first. What he says, goes. The man is simply brilliant."

Pausing, Core tilted his head and listened. He could hear at least four different voices. Raising his fingers, he indicated the number to the men across from them. Both men nodded, pointing to indicate they would take them out.

Core watched as they carefully stepped out of the narrow recess in the wall. On silent feet, they moved down the hallway. Turning into the doorway of the room the men were sitting in, the muffled thud of bullets sounded. Core and Avery stepped around the corner and walked over to the entrance.

One of the task force members was searching the bodies of the men, while the other covered him. On the third body, he pulled out a set of keys and tossed them to Core who caught them in his left hand. Core turned in time to see Avery release a volley of bullets as another guard suddenly appeared around the corner.

A low snarl escaped him when Avery moved cautiously toward the man who was writhing on the floor. She kicked the guard's gun down toward him before she bent over the man and pulled him over onto his back.

"Where is the man that is being held here?" She demanded, holding the weapon in her hand to the man's forehead.

"Down... down... a level," the man muttered, clutching his side.

"How many guards?" She asked.

"Two... Just two," he moaned in a hoarse voice. "I... was sent up here to get the other guys in case..."

"In case what?" Avery asked, a sharp bite in her tone that warned the man he had better be telling her the truth. "In case of what, damn it?"

"In case... the bastard... wakes up," the man choked out. "Please... I need a doctor."

"Stay with him," Core ordered. "The men and I will go after Merrick."

He could tell Avery was about to argue and was surprised when she nodded her head instead. Suspicion darkened his gaze as he stared down at her for several seconds. He finally turned when she raised her eyebrow at him.

"Let's go," Core growled to the two men to follow him.

Core followed the direction that the man Avery had shot came. There was a set of stairs at the far end of the second corridor. Pushing open the door, he stepped cautiously through it. Nodding to the two men, they began to carefully descend downward to the lower floor. Once at the bottom level, Core cast a glance through the small square glass in the door. They wouldn't be able to enter without being seen. He turned to the man on his left side.

"Open the door," he instructed under his breath. "I'll take the right, you two take the left."

Both men nodded in agreement. Raising his hand, he counted down. The officer quickly pulled the door open. Core took the right side, aiming at the two men standing outside of a door at the far in of the hall. The other two men took the left, but it was clear.

Moving cautiously, Core released a satisfied grunt when he discovered the man upstairs had been telling the truth, there had only been the two guards. He pulled the keys out that the task member had thrown him and glanced through the window in the door. Relief and rage mixed together when he saw Merrick's unconscious body chained to a long, narrow bed.

Cursing, he inserted the key into the lock and opened the door. Hurrying forward, he knelt next to the bed and placed his fingers on Merrick's neck. Concern darkened his features and he turned to the two men who stood guard at the door.

"I have to get him back to my world," Core stated. "I do not know what they gave him. Whatever it was, it is affecting his heart. Go back to Avery. Let her know that I have Merrick and have returned to Baade."

"Yes, sir," the officer standing closest to him replied. "We'll notify the rest of the Teams to move in."

Core didn't reply. He inserted another key from the set into the lock in the chain. Soon, he had Merrick free. Pulling his cousin up by his arms, he slung him over his shoulder, grunting at the weight. Balancing himself, he activated the Gateway. Within seconds, he and Merrick had disappeared.

Chapter 18

Addie blinked, looking around at the sterile white walls and dark green curtain. She knew she had fainted earlier. A shudder escaped her when she remembered why. Seeing not one, but two dead bodies up close and personal was more than she could handle, especially with all the blood mixed in with it. It was one thing to see it in a movie or on television, it was an entirely different level to see it in real life.

She grimaced as she sat up. The officers who helped her had called for an ambulance. She had come to as they were depositing her on the stretcher. The paramedics insisted that she be transported to the local hospital after seeing the bruises on her face. Too tired to argue with them, Addie had laid back, closed her eyes, and focused on trying to see if she could feel the strange connection between her and Merrick.

There had been nothing, just as there was nothing now. If anything, the silence was even greater, almost suffocating, in its intensity. Rubbing her left hand on the leg of her jeans, Addie released a tired sigh. It would appear that now that he had been rescued, he didn't need to be in her head any more.

Well, that is just fine, she thought in aggravation. Who needs him anyway?

Addie looked up as a nurse came into the narrow room. The nurse smiled cheerfully at her and handed her a piece of paper. Looking down at it, Addie realized it was a prescription for a mild sedative with instructions on how to take it if she had problems sleeping.

Folding it, she started to slide it into her back pocket when her fingers bumped into soft, folded leather. A relieved sigh escaped her when she realized that her bifold wallet, that she carried while working, hadn't been discovered when she was first captured. Pulling it out, she flicked it open. She had her driver's license, her debit card, and twenty-five dollars in cash.

She nodded absently, not bothering to tell the nurse she couldn't hear a thing the woman was rattling on about. Slipping off the bed, she followed the woman as she stepped out of the small room. Her eyes swept over the busy Emergency room searching for an Exit sign. Signing her thanks, she headed for the bright red sign and freedom.

It took several minutes before she found her way around to the front of the hospital. Stepping out into the late afternoon sun, she waved her hand at a Taxi parked further along the curved drive. Opening the door, she asked the driver to take her to the nearest car rental company.

The driver nodded, looking sympathetically at Addie's bruised and tired face. She sat back and glanced out the window as he drove away from the hospital. A part of her wondered if she was supposed to stick around and give some kind of statement, but the other part of her was too depressed and tired to care. If anyone needed a damn statement, they could come find her.

An hour later, Addie was on the road, heading back to Portland. She had picked up a rental car, stopped at a local bank and dipped into her precious savings account, and headed north. There was no way she would make it all the way home tonight, but she could at least get halfway there.

At midnight, she pulled into a small, mom-and-pop motel, and got a room for the night. She barely remembered staggering down the long, concrete corridor to the end. Using the key with the bright, red plastic tag with the room number on it, she pushed open the door and stepped inside.

She was so tired, that she leaned against the door as she turned the knob to lock it and placed the swinging bar as an added precaution. Turning, she pushed off the door and dropped the key on the small table in front of the air conditioner. She debated whether to get a shower or just crawl into the closest queen size bed.

The bed won when she stumbled as she slipped the soft shoes one of the nurses gave off and found herself sitting on the end of it. Twisting, she crawled up the bed, pulled the covers back far enough to slid underneath them, before pulling the spare pillow into her arms and hugging it to her chest.

Merrick? She thought, focusing and pushing her thoughts out as hard as she could. *Merrick, please, if you can hear me, let me know that you are alright.*

Addie waited several long minutes, hoping and praying for some type of response, some feeling that he might have heard her. A lone tear escaped and ran down over the bridge of her nose when silence continued to plague her. Burying her face in the pillow, she sniffed, and sniffed, and sniffed, but it was no use. The tears that hadn't fallen throughout her ordeal suddenly decided to burst the dam they were behind and flood the pillow she was holding with a torrential wave of salty liquid. It was close to one o'clock in the morning before she finally fell into an exhausted, dreamless sleep.

* * *

Merrick shot upright, snarling loudly as he came awake. His heart thundered in his chest as his eyes whipped around the room. It took a moment for his brain to registered the familiar walls and structure of a healing unit on his world.

Jerking his head toward the window, he breathed in deeply when he saw Core rise out of the chair in front of it. He watched as his cousin and second in command stretched and rubbed the back of his neck. Pulling his gaze away, he searched the room for another body, this one with soft curves and hair the color of the sun.

"Where is she?" He demanded in a voice hoarse with dryness.

"Where is who?" Core asked, stepping over to the small table near the bed and pouring a cup of water. He held it out to Merrick. "Welcome back."

Merrick nodded and reached for the cup. He grimaced when his hand trembled as he took the cool, clear liquid. Drinking deeply, he held it out for more.

"Where is Addie? She was being held with me," Merrick demanded, taking the cup again. "Rockman and the guards took her from me."

"There was a human female, I don't know what happened to her after I came for you," Core stated, taking the cup from Merrick after he drained it again. Setting it down, he looked back at Merrick's pale, drawn face. "We almost didn't get to you in time."

Merrick grimaced as he pulled the pillows up behind him so he could lean back. He felt as weak as a newborn babe. Rubbing his chest, he frowned when he felt the pull of several tubes. Scowling, he looked at the machine next to the bed.

"What happened?" He demanded, waving his hand at the machine. "Why wasn't I placed into a regen bed?"

"You were," Core replied with a raised eyebrow. "It took two days in it just to keep you alive. The damn thing had to practically rebuild your heart. Whatever in the hell the humans shot you with, you had a reaction to it. Five minutes more and you would have been too far gone for even the regen to save you."

"How long have I been unconscious?" Merrick asked grimly, his thoughts turning to Addie.

"Six moon cycles," Core answered, glancing out the window at the darkening sky. "Almost seven."

"The humans?" Merrick asked, leaning his head back and watching Core through half-closed eyes. "What happened to them?"

"The woman we captured was killed," Core responded. "From the security feed RITA was able to get, there was one other male that we know of."

"There are two," Merrick bit out. "One of the males is called Weston. The other is called Markham. Who killed the female? Was it Doctor Rockman?"

"Yes," a cheerful, feminine voice suddenly stated. "I'm not sure who did the actual killing, unfortunately. It would appear Weston realized that something was going on with the security feed and shut everything down. I'll have to talk to RITA to figure out how he knew."

Merrick's eyes widened and Core, who had been about to sit back down in the chair he had been sitting in earlier, twisted with a loud curse. Both men stared in disbelief as a gorgeous, human redhead that looked suspiciously like an older version of Tansy Bell, only slightly translucent, appeared in the room with them.

Merrick stared back into RITA2's dancing green eyes. She was wearing a white lab coat that hid the dress she was wearing underneath it, and a pair of dark green heels. Her dark red hair was piled on top of her head and she appeared to be holding some type of medical tablet. He shook his head and ran a weary hand down over his face as he tried to wrap his brain around how a computer program could suddenly have a body... of sorts.

"DAR, the Baade's newly reprogrammed Defense, Armament, and Response system, and I have been working on developing a four dimensional holographic image. I think we've just about got it figured out," RITA2 chuckled as a pair of dark green glasses with tiny jewels on them suddenly appeared. "Do you think glasses make me look more professional?"

"Glasses?" Core muttered in confusion. "What the hell is going on?"

One of RITA2's delicate, perfectly created eyebrows rose. "I'm checking in on Merrick, of course. I've been added to the medical server. I think the doctors here are just interested in how a human female likes to have sex, that seems to be the most asked question. But, who am I to complain. I usually just direct them to Tilly, since that was not part of my original programming."

Merrick leaned his head back and closed his eyes. He wasn't sure if he was up to dealing with this right now. Opening his eyes, he stared at RITA2 for several long seconds, thinking.

"Do you know what happened to a female named Addie Banks that was being held with me?" He asked in a husky voice.

RITA2's perfectly detailed face went blank for a fraction of a second before she blinked at him. He would have missed the unusual pause if he hadn't been so focused on her answer. A serene smile curved her lips before she answered.

"She was seen at Reno Regional Hospital by Doctor Calvin Hampton, the ER physican. Accessing medical records.... Thank you, RITA, I have them uploaded. Addie Banks, age twenty-two, female,

Caucasian, non-smoker, non-drinker," RITA2 blinked and chuckled. "She isn't very exciting."

"RITA2," Merrick growled in annoyance, sitting forward.

"Oh, yes," RITA2 murmured. "According to the records, she was fine except for some slight bruising to her right cheek and slightly elevated blood pressure. The doctor stated her blood pressure may be due to the circumstances of her captivity. She was released with a prescription for a mild sedative and ordered to take it easy for the next few days. The hospital security cameras recorded her getting into a cab. The cab records show she was taken to a local rental car agency... Oh my," RITA2 murmured.

"What?!" Both Merrick and Core demanded, sitting forward when she paused and a devilish grin curved her bright red lips.

"She lied to the attendant and on the paperwork about her age," RITA2 stated. "The attendant must not have verified it against her driver's license, otherwise they would never have rented her the car. Perhaps, she is more exciting than I originally profiled from her medical records. Mm, I'll have to analyze that later to see if I can reduce the percentage of error."

"RITA2!" Merrick snapped. "Where. Is. Addie?!"

"Oh, she stopped at a motel for the night, used her credit card to fill up three times on the way back to Portland, delivered the rental the next morning, and picked her car up from Keiser the same day," RITA2 finished in a burst of information. "I have no other records of her whereabouts since then."

"I need a Gateway device and the location of her dwelling," Merrick ordered, throwing the covers off of his legs and jerking the small, round micro-injectors from his arm. "I…"

Merrick's words slurred when he stood up and everything tilted to the side. He would have fallen if Core hadn't been so quick. With a low moan, he sat down on the edge of the bed and bowed his head, trying to breathe through the dizziness that clouded his vision.

"Rest for tonight," Core advised. "Why is it so important to get to this female? Did she do something?"

Merrick uncurled his left hand, turning it palm side up. Slowly lifting his head to stare back at Core, he fought to keep from passing out. He needed to get to Addie, but in the shape he was in now, he would be no use to her.

"She is my bond mate," he replied in a drained voice. "She has also captured my heart."

Chapter 19

Addie glanced around her clean apartment. For the past five days since her return to Portland, she had hidden away in it. The first two days she had cried. The third day, she had laid around like something the cat had dragged in and left under the mat. By the fourth day, the silence in her head had been about to drive her insane.

"No more," she growled in a low voice. "I won't ever, *ever* let anyone close to me again. I'm better off alone. He got what he needed. He's gone home, Addie girl. Anyway, he thought too much. There's a reason humans can't talk to each other telepathically—it's called privacy! If I get involved with some alien mind-talking, never-stays-out-of-my head guy, he'll know everything! Just think about the problems that would cause! First of all, I could never win an argument, because he would know what I was going to say. Second, I could never surprise him because he would know the minute I thought of a gift and what it was going to be. Third, I couldn't just think dirty, nasty, hot and horny, how-good-his-ass-looked thoughts without him.... without him... Damn it all to hell! I am *not* going to cry again."

And she hadn't. Instead, she had cleaned her bedroom closet, then under the bed and her dresser drawers. Not stopping, she tackled the dust behind her dresser and even cleaned the blinds. And when she was done with that, she moved on to the tiny bathroom. She continued on to the sitting room and kitchen. Now, she was out of rooms to clean and rubbing her damn left hand on her jeans again when it began to itch.

Glaring at the intricate pattern, she scowled. She needed to get out of her apartment. What she could really use was a walk down to the local coffee shop where she would treat herself to one of their pastries filled with gooey, sugary, delicious cream that melted in her mouth.

Grabbing her black, nylon jacket off the back of the dinette chair, she put it on. She picked up her wallet and keys off the end table by the couch and slid them into her jacket pocket. Starting to pull her long hair out, she paused and glanced out the window.

Her nose crinkled up when she saw that it had begun to rain. With a shrug, it didn't matter. It wasn't like she would melt. Opening the door, she stepped out into the hallway, pulling the door shut behind her. Turning, she slid her key into the deadbolt and turned it.

Her eyes instinctively glanced toward Ted and Pam's empty apartment. Ted had left the day after she got home. He told her that after what happened at Keiser, he and Pam had talked. They were going to go stay with her parents for a while in Seattle. He was going to look for a job near them.

"I'm sorry, Addie," he said, glancing at her. "With a baby on the way, we can't afford to take chances. It could have easily been me instead of Crawford, who had been murdered."

"I understand," Addie had signed. "I'm happy for both of you."

"Have you ever thought of moving further north?" Ted signed, the words flowing from his hands, as well as, his mouth. "I know you have family here, but you never seem to see them all that much, and well, both Pam and I would love it if you wanted to come stay for a while with us once we get settled."

"I'm good," Addie signed. "Still, I'd love to come visit you both. I'm happy for you. You know I love both you and Pam. You two were the only ones who really kept in touch with me after I was sick."

The tears had come again when Ted pulled her into his arms and held her close. It seemed that just when she thought her life was finally working out, fate threw a monkey wrench into it. Now, it felt like it was spiraling out of control.

Addie pushed the depressing thoughts away. Taking the stairs, she pushed open the door to the apartment building and stepped out. Turning left, she pulled up the hood of her jacket to protect her face. Her head bowed, she quickly walked down the sidewalk.

* * *

"Is that her?" The man standing under the awning across the street from the apartment building asked.

"Yeah," the short man next to him replied, watching Addie as she hurried down the street. "Let's go."

The tall man nodded. "I'll call Weston. He said he wanted to know when we found her."

"Fine, I just want to get out of this damn rain," the shorter man mumbled. "I hate this fucking constant cloud-pissing."

The two men squeezed between two cars and jogged across the road. Within seconds, they had slipped into the apartment building. Taking the stairs up to the third floor, they stopped to watch as an elderly woman passed them. It didn't take them long to locate Addie's apartment based on the information Weston had given them. Picking the locks, they both silently slid into her apartment to wait for her.

* * *

"Merrick," Core started to say before he growled in frustration.

"No," Merrick replied.

"You have only been on your feet for a few hours. Let me go with you," Core said in aggravation. "If something happens to you again, the council will go to war with Earth."

"Nothing will happen to me," Merrick snapped. "I will only be gone long enough to get Addie, no longer. Besides, you know the council would not agree to let me return. They are trying to restrict the use of the Gateway devices."

"That is all the more reason I should go with you," Core pointed out. "We can be in and out before the council knows we are gone."

"I need you here, Core," Merrick replied quietly. "There is hope for our clan. I need you to convince the council that we must be able to use Cosmos' Gateway between our worlds. I have found my bond mate. If I can find the one meant for me, it means hope for the other warriors. I will not let the council decide the fate of the Eastern Clan. I made a promise to our people. I will not fail them."

"And if the council still denies us?" Core asked in a strained voice. "What then?"

Merrick looked into his cousin's eyes, just as he had looked into the eyes of the men of their clan the day he had taken over as their leader. He had sworn he would do everything in his power to protect the clan. Part of that promise was the hope of finding more women. He now knew that it was a promise he could keep.

"We only have one device," Merrick murmured. "I need you to keep it safe. I'll have you open the Gateway so I can go through."

"How will I know when to open it again?" Core asked in frustration, running his hand through his hair. "You will be trapped there without one."

"I will do what Addie did before," Merrick replied, sliding several weapons into the pockets of his black pants. This time, he was taking weapons he knew how to use. He would not be caught unprepared again. "I will use her communication device to contact RITA. She will find us, and lock on to our location and pass the information onto RITA2, who will notify you so you can open the Gateway."

Core looked skeptically at Merrick. "How do you know RITA and RITA2 will cooperate," he asked.

"Because, darling. I love a good romance," RITA2 stated, materializing in Merrick's room. "Just to let you know, the council will be convening in three days. You need to make sure you are back by then. Your name was mentioned."

Merrick grimaced. He knew there would be a review of what happened and how it could be prevented from happening in the future. He hated that part of his position. Nodding, he slid several more sharp blades into the sheaths on his boots. Grabbing a long, black leather jacket, he slid his arms into it.

"I am ready. You have it set for Addie's apartment?" He asked, turning to look at RITA2. His lips curved at the corner when he saw that she was wearing a sparkling green fitted dress today with a matching lab coat. "How many warriors have walked into walls today?"

RITA2 chuckled as she processed what he was asking. Since she had first started appearing this way, she had discovered that the unattached Prime warriors, especially the younger ones, had a tendency to try to follow her. While she could pass through walls and unopened doors with ease, they could not. Last night, one of the male nurses attending Merrick had tried to follow her out into the hallway. Unfortunately, he forgot to open the door before he tried to go through it.

"Six, if you count two of the council members," she replied with wicked delight. "DAR is working on his image now. I do believe he is a touch jealous."

"Thank you, RITA2, for your assistance," Merrick said. "My clan will thank you, as will the warriors when they are able to find their mates."

"Be safe," RITA2 replied affectionately. "I'll let my twin know you are coming through and to expect your call."

Merrick nodded. Turning, he grasped Core's forearm and gave a sharp nod before letting go. Soon, soon he would be with Addie again and the painful ache inside him would disappear along with the loneliness.

I'm coming for you, Addie, Merrick thought as the Gateway between the worlds shimmered. *Never again will I leave you alone.*

* * *

Merrick stepped through the Gateway into the lower basement area of the apartment building Addie lived in. RITA2 felt it would be less likely for him to be seen. He rolled his shoulders, and glanced around. A single, dim light lit the interior of the room. There were a series of large metal cabinets along the far wall. Long lists of numbers were printed out and taped to the front. The equipment looked like it might be a heating source. Turning back around, he stepped up to the door and listened before pulling it open.

The door opened under a stairwell and into a small, dim foyer. He had only taken a few steps forward when the door leading into the building opened. His breath caught in his throat when the figure reached up with one hand and pushed the damp hood off her head.

Addie, Merrick whispered.

Addie's blonde head snapped up and her eyes searched the dim interior with a combination of shock and confusion. The moment their eyes connected, a dark scowl swept across her face and her eyes turned a stormy green.

What are you doing here? She demanded, clutching the small plastic bag and a cup of coffee in her hand. *I thought you had returned to wherever you came from.*

I did, he replied, taking a step forward.

Well, you should have stayed there, she muttered, turning away from him and stepping toward the stairs.

Merrick watched in shock as Addie walked away from him. It was not the reception he had been expecting. Following her, he reached for her before grimacing. She had erected a firm wall around her thoughts, closing him out. Taking the steps two at a time, he quickly caught up with her as she reached the landing.

He started to say something, but an elderly female with a small creature on a leash was coming down the stairs. Stepping to the side, he waited impatiently for the woman to pass him on the landing. He glared down at the fluffy white creature when it paused to sniff his boots.

"Mr. Potter won't bite," the woman assured him. "He likes to meet new people."

Merrick grunted, his eyes moving upward to Addie's stiff back. She was moving up to the third level. He needed to catch up with her and make her look at him. She obviously wasn't going to allow him into her mind in the mood she was in right now.

"Are you going to see Addie, too?" The woman asked with a look of disapproval. "She already has two men in her apartment. I just don't know about young women these days. I thought she was such a nice young girl. So quiet and all, if you know what I mean?"

"Two men," Merrick repeated, his eyes jerking down to the old woman. He ignored her startled gasp when she saw the glowing flames in his eyes. "Addie!"

Merrick picked the woman up around the waist and moved her out of his way. Taking the stairs three at a time, he moved with an unnatural speed for a human. He rounded the top of the third floor stairs at the same time Addie stepped into her apartment. Fear boiled over inside him when he heard her loud scream.

Chapter 20

Fury boiled inside Addie as she climbed the steps leading up to her apartment. She had spent the last five days, *five very long frigging days*, coming to terms with the fact that she would never see Merrick again. Just when she felt like she was succeeding, he waltzes back in like nothing had happened, filling the silence in her head back up with his deep, rich voice.

It reminded her of her sister's loser husband and the games he used to play. For three years, Mick would come and go, saying he needed time to discover what he really wanted in life, and for three years, Angie waited. It had almost killed her sister, loving a guy who would treat her so badly. Addie could never understand why her sister would put up with a guy like that, until now.

I don't love him, she growled to herself. *It is lust, caused by the extreme situation we were in. I don't think he is the bravest, sexiest, gentlest man... alien... in the universe.*

Unlocking the door to her apartment, she frowned when she discovered the deadbolt unlocked. Strange, she could have sworn she locked it when she left. Shrugging her shoulders, she pushed open the door. She must have forgotten. As crazy as the last week had been, she was lucky she remembered to even close the damn thing.

She had just tossed the uneaten pastry on the table by the couch when the sudden sense that she wasn't alone swept through her. She turned in time to see two men, one coming out of her bedroom and the other out of the kitchen toward her. A loud scream escaped her. Her eyes registered the gun in the short man's hand as he came out of the kitchen. Not thinking, her hand rose and she threw the contents of her hot coffee at him. The burning liquid struck him in the face, causing him to fall backwards with a loud, angry curse.

Addie twisted on her heel, trying to get back out of the door when a dark, menacing shadow flew through the door. She stumbled to the side as it brushed past her. Off balance, she hit the wall and slid down into an inelegant heap.

Merrick hit the tall, thin man that had been coming out of her bedroom in the stomach. The force of his impact knocked the man backward into the wall next to the bathroom door. She watched in horrid fascination as Merrick grabbed the man's arm when he raised it, the black outline of a handgun in the intruder's grip. For once, Addie was thankful for being deaf when the man's arm suddenly bent at an unnatural angle.

A startled cry escaped her when she felt hard fingers sink into her arm. Turning, she was able to raise her arm in time to deflect the brutal blow aimed for her face. Raising her other hand, she gripped the man's other hand as he tried to drag her back into the kitchen. She grunted in pain when he twisted out of her grasp and wrapped a steel hand around her wrist.

The grip the man had on her arms forced her to roll onto her back. She started to scream again, but he suddenly released her arms and knelt over her. Addie choked when he wrapped his hands around her throat, cutting off the sound.

Struggling, she tried to claw at his arms and face. Remembering what her brothers told her, she raised her knee in an effort to slam it into his groin. The tight hold on her throat lessened for a brief moment, allowing her to draw a desperate breath of air into her starving lungs before the man on top of her trapped her legs and began choking her again.

Dark spots edged her vision momentarily before the weight of the man was lifted off of her. Rolling onto her side, she held a shaking hand to her tender throat even as she pushed up into a sitting position. Horror gripped her when she saw Merrick twist the man's head between his hands. Even though she couldn't hear the sickening snap of his neck, she could see the odd angle of his head as he collapsed onto her sitting room floor.

Another short scream escaped her when Merrick suddenly knelt in front of her. Tearing her eyes off the body of the dead intruder, she looked at him with dazed, frightened eyes. It took a moment for her to realize he was speaking to her.

"Are you hurt?" He asked.

Addie shook her head and gripped his arm as he helped her to stand. Her eyes moved back to the man with the broken neck and over to the taller intruder. He, too, was dead, a knife stuck through his chest. Turning, Addie rushed to the kitchen sink when her stomach rebelled at the sight. She shook her head when Merrick rubbed her back. Right now, she needed a moment alone.

There is not time, Addie, Merrick said in a voice filled with regret. *I hear the sound of alarms.*

Addie didn't answer him. Turning on the water, she quickly rinsed her mouth and in the sink before turning it off. Only when she felt like she wasn't going to throw up again, did she respond.

"They can't find you," she whispered, turning to look at him. "The police.... They can't find you. If the government finds out about you, it will be even worse than Rockman."

Merrick threaded his fingers through her hair and held her tenderly, forcing her to look into his eyes. "Please, do not close me out. I need to be able to talk to you. I need you to hear what I say. These men were here for you, Addie. The other man muttered Weston's name before he died. You are in danger, as well."

Addie's eyes glanced toward her sitting room. Nodding, she hugged her jacket closer to her as a shiver raced through her body. Opening her mind, she felt the familiar touch of Merrick's presence in it. She also felt his concern.

"We can go to Ted and Pam's apartment," she said, pulling her keys out of her pocket. "They have a fire escape outside their bedroom window that leads down to the alley. My car is parked down the street."

"Let's go. There are many footsteps coming up the stairs," Merrick replied grimly with a nod.

Addie quickly picked out the key she would need to unlock the door across the hallway from her apartment. Ted and Pam had given her a key so she could feed their fish whenever they went out of town. Keeping her gaze turned away from the bodies of the dead men, she rounded the corner of the kitchen and hurried out of her apartment. Her hands trembled as she quickly unlocked the door across the hall. Slipping inside, she closed the door just as she caught a glimpse of a black hat on the staircase.

* * *

Merrick followed Addie as she moved through the small apartment that was a mirror image of her own. She walked through the small sitting room to the back bedroom. He watched as she fumbled with the locks on the window before trying to open it. A low, frustrated cry escaped her when she couldn't get it to open. Touching her shoulder, he ran his gaze around the window frame. A small pin had been placed in the top, left corner. Pulling it free, he opened the window.

He carefully stuck his head out, making sure the ally was clear before he turned to Addie. The look of distress on her face tore at him. Unable to bear it, he reached out and slowly drew her into his arms. It took a moment, but she finally relaxed against him and wrapped her arms around his waist.

We must go, he thought with regret as he released her and stepped back. *I hear more footsteps. It will not be long before they will search the alley.*

"Okay," Addie replied. "I'll go first."

"No," Merrick said, placing a hand on her arm. "Let me."

He glanced at her pale, composed face before turning away and climbing out onto the metal platform. Nodding his head, he helped Addie through the window before turning and beginning the short climb down. Once he'd dropped to the concrete below, he turned and caught Addie around the waist.

"To the right," she murmured. "We can come up further down the street so it doesn't look like we came from here."

Merrick's admiration for Addie grew when she turned and began walking rapidly away from the apartment building. He could feel her fear and confusion, but he could also feel her determination.

You are an amazing female, Addie, Merrick couldn't resist telling her.

Heat swept through him when she glanced over her shoulder and rolled her eyes at him. This was the Addie he knew. The one that would not give up, no matter what was happening.

Don't you believe it, she growled back, pausing at the corner of the building for a brief moment before nodding to him. *You made me cry! I don't like crying.*

A chuckle escaped Merrick when she crinkled her nose at him and glared before hurrying over to the a dark blue transport. He would have to remember that she didn't like to cry, he thought as he climbed into the passenger side.

Chapter 21

Addie glanced in the rearview mirror again. So far, it didn't appear that anyone was following them. Neither she, nor Merrick, had spoken to each other since they got in her car. Glancing again, she turned on her blinker and turned another corner.

She had no idea where they were going, she just knew she needed to get away. It wasn't until she had been driving for fifteen minutes that she suddenly realized she had subconsciously headed in the direction of her parent's cottage house. Turning on her blinker again, she sped up and merged with the highway traffic heading northwest on Highway 26.

"Where are you taking us?" Merrick asked, happy that Addie had listened to him and not closed him off.

"My parents have a place outside of Seaside. We call it the Cottage," she responded in a husky voice. "No one will be there right now."

"We need to contact the number you called before," Merrick said, using both his voice and his thoughts. Something told him that while Addie couldn't 'hear' him, she could somehow sense that he was speaking aloud and it gave her comfort. "Core will open the Gateway between our two worlds."

"I don't have my cell phone," Addie replied in a tense voice. "I left it charging in my bedroom. I wasn't expecting to be attacked again."

Merrick felt her pulling away from him. Reaching out, he touched the faint outline of bruising beginning to form on her throat. He pulled back when she pulled away from him. Clenching his fingers into a fist, he let his hand drop.

Addie knew she had shut him out again. Right now, she couldn't deal with anything else. Focusing on the traffic, she switched lanes and accelerated.

Her mind churned with questions, doubts, and confusion. Who were those men and what did they want with her? Merrick had said the tall man had mentioned Weston. Did Weston think she might know where Merrick was? Or was he just following through with his threat to rape her? She wouldn't put it past the guy. The man had some serious mental issues and needed to be locked up himself.

Then, there were the questions about why Merrick came back. She was thankful he had or she would probably be dead, or worse, by now. Could wherever he came from, see the future and he just wanted to save her because she had saved him? Did he need more help from her? That seemed unlikely considering there had been another of his kind among the rescuers back in Reno.

Did he... Does he think he owes me some kind of explanation before he disappears again? This time forever, she wondered, glancing at his stiff face.

Pulling her eyes back to the road in front of her, she refused to think he came back because he felt sorry for her, or because of their one, brief sexual encounter. Perhaps, he wanted to tell her that he was sorry.

God, I hope he doesn't try to apologize and tell me it was a mistake, done just to save our lives, she thought with a sinking feeling.

Addie rubbed her left palm against her left leg as it tingled. Her eyes flickered to Merrick when she saw him jerk and glance briefly at her before he turned his head to look out the window. Raising her hand to her lips, she pressed the center of her palm to her lips and licked the center of the pattern with her tongue.

A frown creased her brow and her eyes flickered to Merrick again when he shifted in his seat, as if he was uncomfortable. Addie figured he might be, considering that his long legs were jammed into a narrow area. Pulling her hand away from her mouth, she tightened her lips to keep from making his life any easier. As petty as it was, she was still pissed that he made her cry.

With a groan of exasperation at herself, the pettiness lasted thirty seconds before her conscience kicked in. He had just saved her life. The least she could do was give him more leg room for the last hour of the drive.

"There's a bar under the seat in the front," she said, breaking the silence. "If you pull it up, the seat will slide back and give you more leg room."

Addie's lips curved upward when the seat moved backward and a look of relief swept over Merrick's face. There was just something about the guy that totally got under her skin. He was big, he was tough, he was an alien! But, he was also thoughtful, protective, possessive, tender, gentle,…

That is because you are mine, Addie, Merrick inserted, making her realize that she had opened herself up to him again.

Addie groaned and rolled her eyes. *Tenacious, hard-headed, has a one track mind,* she added.

I like your first descriptions better, Merrick chuckled. *Especially the tender and gentle ones. I will always be tender and gentle with you.*

"You left without any word," she replied in a husky voice. "For six days. The silence…"

Her throat tightened as she remembered the overwhelming silence. It was unlike what she had experienced when she lost her hearing. This was as if a part of her soul had been carved out and was missing.

"Core returned me to my world. I was close to death," Merrick explained. "The drugs Rockman used the last time… I had a reaction to it. Even with the technology on Baade, I came close to not returning for you."

"Oh, Merrick!" Addie exclaimed, feeling horrible for her selfish thoughts. "I'm so sorry. I thought… I didn't think you wanted to come back. I couldn't blame you, not after everything that was done to you."

"What happened to you? After they took you from me?" Merrick asked in a husky voice. "Did Rockman hurt you?"

"No, she was going to… She wanted your…." Addie's face flamed as she remembered just what the horrible woman wanted. "No, the people I called came and rescued me. They left someone to guard me and he was killed. I didn't even know. He had shut me in one of the offices and I fell asleep."

* * *

Merrick could hear the horror, sorrow, and the pain in her voice. Reaching his left hand over, he brushed the silky strands of her hair back behind her ear. Addie reached up and grabbed his hand, pulling it around to her lips. A shudder ran through them both when she pressed a kiss to the center of his palm, right over the mating mark.

"What?" She asked in surprise, releasing his hand and glancing at him.

"The mark is another connection between us," Merrick chuckled again. "Watch."

He raised his left palm to his mouth. Gently blowing warm air across it first, he touched the tip of his tongue to the center and ran the moist tip across it. Addie's loud gasp and startled cry echoed through his mind. It took a moment for him to realize that the transport was slowing down and she was pulling off the side of the road.

He watched as she put the vehicle into park and rested her forehead against the steering wheel. It was several minutes before she sat back, still staring out the front window. She finally looked down at her left palm.

A sense of apprehension filled him when he saw her slowly lift it to her mouth. His hand reached out, wrapping around her wrist to stop her. He waited until she turned to stare into his eyes.

"Addie," he murmured in a voice filled with husky warning.

"I want to see," she whispered.

Merrick drew in a deep breath, steeling himself for what was to come. Nodding, he released her wrist. He should have known better when he saw the glint of amusement and her raised eyebrow as she raised her palm to her lips.

A low moan escaped him when the tip of her tongue teased the symbol, running in a slow circle. He felt the tension growing and stiffened his shoulders when she gently blew a breath of cool air across it. He swore it felt like she was touching his cock.

Sweat beaded on his brow when she scraped her teeth against the mark. He opened his mouth to warn her again at the same time as she stuck out her tongue, pausing to give him a look that suggested he better not say a word. Her eyes lit up when he snapped his lips together in a tight line.

This could get very interesting, she teased.

Or very dangerous, he muttered. *Addie, Gods breath, you are going to make me come in my pants like a lad!*

Addie's silent chuckle echoed in his mind as she continued to scrape, lick, rub, and blow on the mating mark. When she appeared satisfied, he breathed a sigh of relief, fighting the urge to adjust himself. Unable to leave it at her teasing, he reached over and wrapped his hand around the back of her head.

Pulling her toward him, he captured her lips with his, thrusting his tongue through her parted lips and kissing her deeply. His other hand came up to tangle in her hair. He would never get enough of her.

Breaking the kiss, he rested his forehead against hers for a moment as they both tried to catch their breath. He stroked his thumb against her temple. Wishing they were anywhere but here at the moment. He hurt!

Addie's giggle showed that she'd caught his discomfort. A wry grin curved his lips as he released her and sat back in his seat. It was good to hear her laughter.

"We'd better get moving," she said in a husky voice. "The sooner we get there, the sooner we can take care of the ache we are both feeling."

"Goddess' blood, Addie, you are going to kill me," Merrick whispered hoarsely as an image of the two of them tangled around each other filled his mind. "How much further?"

Addie laughed, checking the mirror before pulling back onto the highway. "Thirty minutes, give or take," she replied. "We will need to get some food. This little adventure is killing my savings," she added with a disgruntled sigh.

"I will care for you from now on," Merrick said with a shrug. "You will have no need for your savings."

Addie frowned, but didn't say anything. Instead, she asked him questions about his home and family. All too soon, they were entering the city limits of Seaside, Oregon. It was a small tourist town, but it had retained the family atmosphere of those who had homes along the coast.

Addie pulled into the local grocery store parking lot and pulled into a space. Reaching into the pocket of her jacket, she breathed a sigh of relief that she still had her wallet on her. She touched Merrick's arm when he started to reach for the door handle.

"You need to stay here," she said. "It is too dangerous for you to go with me. From a distance, you look almost human, but from close up, it is easy to see that you are different. I won't be long."

Merrick frowned before giving her a brief nod. "Be careful."

"I will. I'll leave the keys in the ignition in case you need to roll the windows down," she said, opening the driver's door and stepping out. "Is there anything you would like?"

Merrick shrugged. "I will eat most things," he replied.

"Okay, I'll be back in a few," Addie said, shutting the door.

Merrick watched Addie as she grabbed a metal cart from between some yellow metal poles. His eyes roamed her figure as she hurried across the parking lot. Turning his attention back to his surroundings when she disappeared inside the store, he studied the humans coming and going from the store, trying to sense if any of them could be a threat.

Settling back to wait, he ran through what happened earlier. It was clearly evident that Weston hadn't given up. The question was, had Markham?

From the briefing RITA2 and Core had given him, neither man had been caught. The attack on Addie earlier just proved that the men were not only out there, they were close.

Something told him this would not be the last time they would meet up with them. What he didn't know was if Markham was a part of the earlier attack or only Weston. Personally, he didn't care. He planned on hunting both humans down and killing them.

There was also the concern about how Weston, Markham, and Rockman had known that Cosmos' teams were getting close. According to Core, he was moved, sometimes just hours, before a raid. RITA2 stated that all her analyses came back with the same answer: there was a traitor somewhere within the links, either from a member of Cosmos' team or from the government.

"RITA has run a detailed security scan on all of Cosmos' teams, and it came back negative," RITA2 had stated. "My bet is the leak is on the government side. I am still gathering data on all personnel that are involved."

Merrick was more inclined to agree with RITA2. Something wasn't right. This was more than just a chance encounter with Markham that led to his being captured.

He sat up when he saw Addie pushing the cart out of the store. The sunlight caught in her hair and turned it to a shimmering yellow-gold. The bruising on her face had faded, but even with it, he still thought she was the most beautiful female he had ever seen.

Addie's laughter echoed through his mind and he could see the grin on her face as she pushed the cart between the yellow poles before grabbing several bags out of it. He waited as she opened the back of the transport and placed the bags in the back.

"You are so cute," she murmured before pressing the button to close the hatch.

"Cute?" Merrick repeated with a scowl. "Prime warriors are not cute."

More laughter filled the vehicle as Addie slid into the driver's seat. Bending toward him, she wrapped her hand around his nape and pulled him close enough to press a hard kiss to his lips. When she pulled back, her eyes were dazed and her lips swollen and pink.

"Yes, they can be," she said, turning on the engine and pulling out of the parking lot.

Chapter 22

Markham watched as his brother glanced down at the report he had handed to him. Flicking through it, he knew when Weston paused on the property listings. From the previous files, he had decided that Addie Banks wouldn't run to her family. Just the little time he had observed her showed that she would run as far away from them as she could, rather than endanger them.

"She went to Seaside," Markham stated, settling into the chair across from Weston and lighting a cigar.

"She didn't go alone either," Weston muttered. "You saw the police report. There is no way she could have killed the two men we sent in, especially with the injuries and cause of death."

"He's back," Markham reflected, blowing a smoke ring.

Cigars were his Achilles heel, which is why he only allowed himself to have one once a month. This one, he had been saving to celebrate having a new creature mounted in his office. He might have to bend the rule and have two.

"What are we going to do?" Weston asked, setting the file down on the table. "Do you want to send in more men after him?"

"No...," Markham said slowly, glancing up at the ceiling, his eyes following the smoke ring as it dissolved. "No, this time we go. I'll draw him away." He lowered his head and stared into his younger brother's eyes. "I want you to kill the girl and leave her on display for him."

"He isn't going to like that," Weston said with a cruel smile. "Do you think you can give me a little time to have some fun as well?

"Long enough if you don't get a cramp in your dick," Markham replied.

"What do you plan to do then?" Weston asked. "If he cares about the bitch, he will be like hunting a wounded lion."

"There is no fun hunting an animal that doesn't know he is being hunted. I want him mean, desperate, and hungry, so when I kill him, it will be all the more satisfying," Markham pointed out. "Have the helicopter readied."

Weston nodded. "When do you want to go in?" He asked.

"Before daylight," Markham said after a few minutes. "Perhaps a night of fucking will help give him an incentive."

Markham leaned his head back and drew in a deep breath, enjoying the tangy flavor of the Cuban cigar. Exhaling, he blew a series of smoke rings, watching as each floated upward before vanishing. Yes, the idea of inflaming the alien before he killed, sent a shaft of excitement through him.

I hope my taxidermist doesn't mind a more exotic specimen, he thought. *The man really is good and I'd hate to have to find another one.*

* * *

Addie pulled up in front of the house. It was large, roomy, and bright. She smiled at Merrick as she turned off the SUV. It was a place filled with lots of happy memories. Even after her illness, she loved coming here.

"This is my favorite place to come to when I'm feeling lonely," she said with a self-conscious smile. "There is just something so peaceful about being near the water and all the trees and wildlife."

"It is beautiful," Merrick agreed, glancing out the front window of the transport.

"Come on, let's get the groceries inside and I'll show you around," she said, pushing the door open and sliding out. Merrick slid out the other side and walked around the back. "Mom and Dad always leave the utilities on in case one of us kids decide to come up," she added as she pressed the button to open the back hatch.

Addie grinned when Merrick grabbed all the bags of groceries before she could. Pressing the button, she shut the hatch door and locked the car. Walking up the steps to the front door, she searched the keys on her keychain for the correct one. Pulling open the screen door, she inserted the key into the lock and soon was leading him through the living room to the kitchen.

She opened the refrigerator and grinned. Her brothers must have been here recently, it was full of beer and wine. Quickly storing the items that needed to be refrigerated, she opened the freezer. Yep, the guys had been here. There were a couple of steaks in the freezer and some ice cream.

Addie took the steaks out and laid them on the counter. It was still early and they would have time to defrost. She quickly put away the canned goods. A blush rose over her cheeks when she bent over and 'heard' Merrick's soft rumble of appreciation.

Turning, she leaned against the counter. "Knock it off," she teased.

"I want to take it off… All of it off of you," Merrick said, stepping closer to her. "I want you, Addie."

Addie tilted her head back, closing her eyes as he threaded his fingers through her hair on each side. Her hands moved on their own accord, sliding up his chest to wind around his neck. Her eyes slowly opened and she looked up into his blazing silver eyes.

"I think I'm falling in love with you," she whispered.

"I know I am in love with you, Addie," Merrick replied. "You came into my life and refused to leave, even when I wanted you to. You have a hidden strength, in here," he murmured, dropping one of his hands to touch her over her heart, "that all warriors wish they could have."

"You took the silence away," she admitted. "I'm not alone anymore."

"Even if I think too much?" He teased.

Addie laughed, rising up on her toes. "Even if you think too much."

Addie met Merrick halfway as he started to lower his head. The teasing that started in the car ignited a slow burn that just needed the right time to burst into life. What began as teasing soon turned into a flurry of hands trying to touch everywhere at once.

"Merrick," Addie moaned when he ran a series of kisses down along her cheek and neck. "My bedroom is upstairs, second door on the left."

Addie was thankful Merrick didn't need any more encouragement. Wrapping her arms around his neck when he swung her up into his arms, she pressed hot, delicious kisses along his neck. A sense of excitement filled her when his arms tightened possessively around her.

She murmured distracted directions to him when he paused outside of the kitchen. It didn't take long for him to figure out where to go. Turning into her bedroom, she raised her eyes and thanked her parents for giving each of their kids a queen size bed.

Merrick laid her down on her bed, half kneeling, half standing over her. The look in his eyes sent a wave of heat through Addie that pooled between her legs and made her move restlessly against the soft covers.

"Do you have other clothing here?" He asked.

"Of course," Addie responded with a puzzled expression that changed to shocked when he gripped her top and tore it down the middle. "Wow!"

* * *

Merrick was shocked at the primitive urge flowing through him. His hunger for Addie made him do things he never would have considered doing with any other female. All he could think about was taking her over and over. The teasing from earlier, combined with their heated kisses and frantic exploration downstairs, had turned him on until his body hummed with barely controlled restraint.

Staring down at the rapid rise and fall of Addie's breasts and the creamy flesh that was barely covered thanks to the ripped remains of her shirt; he realized what little restraint he had, was gone. Bending over her, he snapped the front of the bra.

Now, this was more like it, he thought as the full mounds flowed and swelled in his hands. He liked big breasts.

You and every other guy I've ever met, she teased.

You have too many clothes on, he growled.

"So do you," she pointed out, looking up and down his body as he bent over her. "I want you, Merrick."

Merrick heard the small wobble in Addie's voice. His eyes jerked up to hers, before they darkened again at the hot desire reflected in her gaze. Gripping the bottom of his shirt, he yanked it over his head and threw it to the side. His boots and pants soon followed.

His hand shot out and pressed Addie back when she started to sit up and reach for him. He shook his head. He was too close to the edge. It was taking everything in him not to scare her with his desire.

"Go ahead and scare me," Addie whispered. "I think I can take it."

"Addie," Merrick warned, fisting his cock in his hand. "I want you. I want you very badly."

He watched as Addie's eyes moved down to his hand. If she wasn't careful, she might get what she was asking. The few times he had been so close to the edge, he had used restraints. He had none here and he seriously doubted that Addie would.

A hissing breath escaped him when Addie's hands went to the waistband of her jeans. She unbuttoned them before slowly pulling the zipper down. She kicked her white leather shoes off her feet before rising her ass up just far enough of the bed to slid her jeans and dark red panties down. Once they were at her ankles she raised her legs to pull them off.

That was the moment that Merrick knew he was lost. The control he had been keeping on his emotions snapped. Four months of captivity, combined with his fear that something might happen to Addie, broke through all of his resistance, splintering it into a million unrecognizable pieces.

Merrick yanked the jeans and panties off of Addie's ankles, while keeping her legs up. Wrapping a hand around each delicate calf, he pulled her until her ass was on the edge of the bed. Spreading her, he aligned his cock with her moist curls. Tightening his grip on her ankles until they were at his waist, he slowly released them.

"Are you sure of this, Addie?" he demanded in a tight voice. "Are you very sure?"

"Yes," she said, never looking away. "Yes, I'm very, very sure."

Merrick didn't give her a chance to finish her sentence. Surging forward, he impaled his cock deep inside her. Bracing his arms on either side of her, he pulled out and pushed back in, giving her every inch of his cock.

"Yes," he groaned as he began rocking back and forth.

He could feel Addie's soft moans as he tilted his hips, trying to go even deeper. The feel of her gripping his cock in a tight, slick fist was almost agonizing in the pleasure it gave him. Wrapping his arms around her, he bent his knees until they were pressed up against edge of the bed. He held her tight, as he continued to drive into her. Each stroke took him closer to the precipice where he could lose himself in her.

Lowering his face to her shoulder, he ran long, frantic kisses along it to her neck. This is what it was to have a female who meets him with as fierce a passion as he had. Her hands were running over his back and sides, kneading while her legs locked him to her as if she was terrified he would suddenly disappear.

Rising up, he pulled her arms away from him. He wanted to see her stretched out before him. Pulling her arms up over her head, he held them there, gazing down at her as he drove into her hot core.

"Admit you are my mate," he growled, not pausing. *Admit it.*

Admit that you are mine, she said defiantly. *Promise me that you won't let me go and that you won't leave me.*

Never! Merrick promised. *Never, Addie.*

Then, yes, she admitted, shattering around him with a loud cry.

Yes! Merrick hissed, closing his eyes and bowing his head when his body answered her call.

He could feel the pulsing jets of his seed filling her. The hot fluid washing both of them in his essence. Something told him that he needed to mark her, prepare her womb to accept the prize she had demanded, that he was her mate.

Bending forward, he opened his eyes, a red haze of desire blurring his vision. All he could think of was that he needed to prepare her for their mating. He barely heard her gasp or felt her struggles as she tried to break free of the grip he had on her hands.

Merrick, Addie whispered, staring at his teeth. *Merrick…*

I am yours, Addie, Merrick whispered through her mind. *Just as you will forever be mine.*

A low rumble escaped him as he sunk his teeth into the top of her left breast. Her scream turned to a moan as the chemical in his bite ignited her already heightened sense. He carefully pulled back as her struggles lessened and the desperate rocking of her hips registered.

Merrick released her hands and slid his arms around her, supporting her as he stood with her legs wrapped around his waist. Walking from the bottom of the bed to the side, he lowered them both down again until he was lying on it with her on top of him. He had never had a woman ride him before, but the images in Addie's mind would not let him ignore the possibility.

Ride me, Addie, Merrick ordered, lifting his hands to cup her breasts. *Ride me.*

Chapter 23

Merrick smiled, wrapping his arm around Addie's waist when she leaned against him. The sun was beginning to set and she had wanted to go for a walk along the beach. He closed his eyes, breathing in the salty smell.

If his body wasn't so satiated, he would almost think he had imagined this afternoon. Nothing in his experience had prepared him for the explosive passion. Opening his eyes, he glanced down at Addie's golden hair. She was real.

"Of course, I'm real," she chuckled, tilting her head back to look at him. "Why would you think I wasn't?"

"The females on Baade are not...," Merrick paused, looking back out at the ocean. "There are few females on our world. Most have been chosen through the mating rites ceremony. The ones still unmated and not of age are either protected fiercely by their clans or sent to an island holding where they are kept safe."

"What do you mean 'kept safe'?" Addie asked, turning and wrapping her arms around him. "Why would they be in danger?"

"Desperation can cause even the strongest warrior to make poor decisions. In the past, some warriors have taken females that were not their bond mates," Merrick explained, pausing for a moment before continuing. "Our scientists are searching for the reason why fewer and fewer female children have been born over the last few centuries. It has reached a critical level where the number of males far exceeds that of the females. There are other species, but none have been capable of being a bond mate, until Tink Bell appeared through the Gateway Cosmos Raines invented. This Gateway connected our two worlds and gave us hope."

"But, are you saying, you've never been with a woman before?" Addie asked in disbelief.

"No," Merrick replied, flushing. "I have been with several females before."

"Oh," Addie said, crinkling her nose up. "I think this is one of those questions best left unasked."

"So do I," he mumbled.

He did not want her to know of some of the females he had bedded when he was younger. Two had been older Prime females who had never had a bond mate and sought comfort with the males. Most of the females had been from off-world. Some had been pleasant enough, while others might have been enough to take the edge off of his lust, they had done nothing for him otherwise. In truth, the last few years, he had buried himself in the life of his clan or taken care of his own wants.

"Addie," he said, looking back down at her with a serious expression. "Tomorrow, I will be returning to my world."

Shock and hurt flashed across her face before she turned it away from him. He knew immediately what she was thinking. He caught a glimpse of it before she tried to shut him out. He was getting better at slipping under her defenses. Raising his hand, he cupped her chin in it so he could turn her back around to face him.

"Okay," she said, trying to avoid his gaze.

"I must return before the council is aware I am gone," he continued in a quiet tone. "I will not be returning alone. I will be taking you with me."

"Taking me… to your world… as in someplace that isn't Earth?" Addie whispered in shock.

"Yes."

"But, what about my family? I can't just disappear. My mom and dad. My brothers and my sisters," Addie said, shaking her head. "I know I don't see them often, but we always know we are there if we ever need each other. I can't hurt them like that."

"I will make sure that you see them again," Merrick promised, sliding his hand along her cheek. "It is only right that I inform your parents that I am your mate. It will be vital that they do not tell any others of our existence and I will not be able to share how we travel between the two worlds."

He could see the hope flash across Addie's face. He knew it was a lot to ask of her, but the possibility of living with him among the Eastern Mountains was too important. Concern and a small amount of fear coursed through him when she bit her lip and looked up. Indecision pulled at her, and he could hear the question in her thoughts.

"What is it?" He asked, seeing her hesitancy.

"Do you have Massage Therapists on your world?" She asked.

"I am not sure what a Massage Therapist is, but if you wish to do it, I will do whatever I can to help you," he promised.

"Oh, Merrick," Addie cried out, throwing her arms around his neck. "Maybe this can work."

Lifting her up and holding her tightly in his arms, Merrick buried his face in her neck. He didn't care what he had to do, he would never let her go. In just the few days they had known each other, he had discovered the piece of his heart he hadn't realized was missing until he met her.

..*

"I could take them both out now," Weston commented, looking through the scope of his rifle at the couple on the beach.

"No," Markham replied, looking through his as well. "I want him to know who is going to kill him."

"We won't have long once the girl is officially reported missing," Weston said, lowering his rifle and turning to sit back against the log. "The last report we received from your source stated the police are searching for her. One eyewitness, who has been considered not credible, stated she saw Banks and a man with glowing silver eyes, head up to her apartment right before there were loud screams. She was the one who called them."

"We will be long gone by the time they search for her here," Markham replied with a shrug, lowering his gun and standing up. He watched as his brother stood with a wince. "How's your shoulder?"

"Fine," Weston bit out, shifting the rifle to his good shoulder and looking around. "Let's get back to the car. I want to go over the blueprints to the house again."

Nodding, Markham glanced one more time to the faint outline of the two figures. A smile curved his lips. It would be interesting to see just how good the alien was when he wasn't drugged up.

* * *

Merrick watched as Addie prepared a salad to go with the steaks that were on the small, propane grill outside. He swore she kept bending over just so she could tease him. Every time she did, a low, unconscious rumble of approval escaped him.

I want her again, he thought, glancing at the steaks, then back at her again trying to determine if they could just skip the meal and get straight to the lovemaking.

"No, we can't skip it," Addie chuckled, picking up the two bowls and setting them on the table. "I'm starving. I'll make you a deal, you feed me, then you can love me all you want."

Merrick reached out and wrapped his arms around Addie's waist and brushed a brief, hard kiss across her lips. Pleasure and warmth spread through him when she softened and returned his kiss. Opening his mind to her, he let her feel his emotions.

I never thought to feel like this, or that I would want to open myself to my mate should I find her, Merrick admitted reluctantly.

Why? Addie asked, really enjoying that she could 'hear' his voice.

I always believed it would make me vulnerable, he confessed. *My mother was killed when she was down at the river. She slipped, striking her head, and drowned before my father could reach her. I was but a young boy, but I remember watching my father fade away before my eyes. I was determined to keep my own thoughts and feelings separate from my bond mate if I ever found her.*

But...? She asked, tears blurred her vision as she saw the images in her head of a beautiful woman standing near a handsome older warrior.

But, I was not prepared for what it would mean to really love someone, he said. *The feeling of being whole, of being never alone...*

Of never being surrounded by an empty silence, Addie finished for him.

For the first time, he felt the weight of loneliness that Addie had endured for years, the constant silence. He thought of what it would mean to lose his hearing after having it, just the simple things he took for granted. The sound of his niece, Nadine's laughter and endless questions, his aunt, Nadu's, gentle rebukes when he tried to steal one of her fresh pastries, even the joking of the warriors as they trained or hunted.

I miss the sound of music and the birds, even the sound of the wind and the ocean, Addie murmured, pulling away from him. *I miss that I will never hear the sound of my children's laughter.*

Addie, Merrick began to say, stopping when she shook her head.

I've finally come to terms with it, she said. *Can you check the steaks? They should be ready.*

Yes, Merrick replied with a nod.

* * *

"Trudy," Rose said, scanning the data coming in. "We've got a problem."

"What?" Trudy asked, looking up from the computer screen she was studying.

"I think I've found a snitch," Rose bit out in a hard voice.

"Our leak? It isn't Runt, I hope. I still haven't found her," Trudy complained. "Even RITA hasn't been able to pick up anything! I swear, it is like the girl totally vanished off the face of the Earth. Hell, I didn't think she would be able to stay disconnected this long."

"No, it isn't Runt. It looks like one of the President's aides has been having a sudden financial boom," Rose replied, studying the data in front of her. "Damn."

"What?" Trudy asked in frustration.

""There was an attack on Addie Banks this morning. She is missing and two men were found dead in her apartment. One with a knife through his chest, and the other with a broken neck."

"Something tells me that not all the aliens are gone," Trudy muttered, reading the police report.

"No, Merrick has returned for Addie," RITA replied. "My sis asked me to wait for his call and let her know so she could lock onto him. Core is on the other side waiting to open the Gateway, but so far, I haven't received a call from him or Addie yet."

Rose groaned and scooted over so Trudy could wheel her chair up next to her. They both scanned the report. Rose had tapped into the phone companies' records and was looking at the text messages sent. Sure enough, short, cryptic messages, some just hours before a raid, had been sent to a series of different numbers.

"Damn it," Rose cursed.

"Look at the last one, Rose," Trudy said, pointing to the screen.

"Shit," Rose snapped out in a frustrated voice.

"RITA…" Trudy mumbled.

"I already have the flight plan uploaded. The helicopter will be ready. I anticipated that you would be flying it, Trudy. Do you want me to activate a team?" RITA asked.

"No," Rose replied grimly. "We don't want to take a chance of the asswipe getting news that we know about him. We are going to have to split up for this one. I'll notify Cosmos while you go warn Merrick. Damn, I wish Avery hadn't gone off the grid just yet. Cosmos has returned to Baade. He and Terra are working on something, but I can still send messages through RITA and RITA2."

"She said it would only be for a couple of days. She deserves a day or two off every few years.,"

Trudy joked, rising out of her seat. "Besides, we can handle this. Just be careful, Rose, or Avery will be hell to live with for a while."

"You too," Rose said. "RITA, I need the corporate jet readied for Washington."

"Already done, Rose," RITA replied cheerfully. "I was wondering why Merrick hadn't contacted me yet, now I know. Ah, love."

Neither woman responded as they geared up. Trudy would take the helicopter to Seaside. RITA would arrange to have a car waiting for her. She would head out to the address the snitch had posted.

At first, they thought they would only be dealing with Addie Banks. Now, they knew there would be a Prime warrior, as well. They weren't sure who the snitch was sending the information to. That would be up to Rose to try to find out. The main thing was making sure that Merrick did not get captured again.

Chapter 24

Addie sighed as the warm water washed over her. Her thoughts were swirling faster than a hamster in a spinning wheel. It was hard to believe in that in less than two weeks, her life could change so dramatically.

She turned when the glass door to the shower opened and Merrick stepped inside. For a moment, she swore her heart skipped a beat at the beauty of his body. Her hand impulsively reached out to touch him.

No, I'll never get enough of this, she thought.

I hope not, Merrick replied in a husky voice. *You have no idea of what this feels like to a Prime male. To have a female so responsive on her own is a wondrous thing.*

Really? She asked in surprise. *Why would the women of your world not want to be touched?*

I am beginning to wonder that myself, Merrick muttered in a hoarse voice.

Addie could tell he was enjoying her touching him. Deciding this gave her the perfect opportunity to both explore his body further and bring him pleasure, she picked up the bar of soap and lathered her palms. A shiver went through her when he moaned again.

I can see your thoughts, he choked out. *I…*

Will just enjoy this, Addie finished, setting the soap back in the soap dish.

Yes, he hissed as she began running her hands over his chest, slightly above his nipples.

Addie concentrated on what she was feeling as she stroked him. Her hands slid over his warm flesh, feeling the hard muscles underneath her palms. The last four years, she had been learning about the anatomy of the human body. While he wasn't human, his physical appearance was similar enough.

She could feel the thick ropes of muscle and used what she had learned to lightly massage them as she explored. One of the things she had done during her studies was strengthen the muscles in her hands so that she could use them and her own body weight. Taking her time, she gently caressed him.

"Addie," he groaned.

A gentle chuckle escaped her at his muttered groan. She glanced up, noting that he was watching her. Licking her lips, she sent an image of her following her hands with her mouth.

You know, you say my name a lot with nothing else behind it, she teased.

I... have trouble thinking in complete sentences when you touch me, he admitted. *How long must I stay still?*

I've just started! Give me at least five minutes, she laughed.

I am counting down the time, he warned. *In five minutes, I will be buried deep inside you.*

Wow, she breathed.

Turning her focus back to his chest, she noted that he didn't have any hair on it. His muscles were thicker, denser than a humans. She suspected that his bones would be as well. Unable to resist, her gaze followed the line of soap bubbles as they moved downward.

His stomach gave a whole new meaning to the words 'six pack abs'. For a moment, she was a little embarrassed by her own soft belly. It could never be called firm.

Don't, he said sharply. *I have no desire to touch hardness. When I touch you, you are soft and melt in my arms. I can hold you and love you, and your curves make me want to explore you. I find it very... sexy.*

Addie glanced up, tilting her head to the side as the water of the shower flowed down on them. A soft, pleased smile curved her lips. The one good thing about talking this way was she knew he was telling her the truth and not just saying something to make her feel better.

I could never lie to you. You would know the moment I did. Plus, it would not be wise. There should not be lies between mates. It would be too dangerous. Besides, my body cannot lie about how you affect me, he added.

Addie nodded, looking down. That was definitely the truth, she thought. His cock was straining upward, as if begging for her attention. Reaching for the soap again, she picked it up and lathered her hands.

This time, she ran her hands over his stomach before slowly sinking down to her knees on the smooth tile. She ran her hands around his heavy balls, enjoying the explosion of feeling from him. Taking her time, she rolled them tenderly between her fingers.

He had no hair here either, just creamy flesh that begged to be caressed. Addie looked up at him as she wrapped one hand around his long, thick cock. Stroking it back and forth, she watched as the flames in his eyes ignited and the silver turned to a dark, liquid color.

You are so beautiful, she whispered before opening her mouth and sliding the tip slowly past her lips.

Goddess, Addie! Merrick moaned, leaning forward and bracing his arms against the wall behind her.

* * *

Merrick thought he was prepared for just about anything when they made love, but nothing prepared him for the erotic sight of Addie's sweet lips wrapped around his cock. They had made love several times and he did not believe it could get any better.

Her passionate responses to his touch, her willingness to allow him to drink her sweet come, and the different positions! Goddess, he didn't know that a female could enjoy the things he had only dreamed of trying. When he had come upstairs after checking to make sure the transport and house were secure, he had heard the sound of water. Seeing Addie's lush figure through the clear glass, the droplets of water coursing down her body, had stirred the need inside him once again. He had quickly shed his clothes and joined her.

"I'm glad you did," she murmured.

Merrick didn't reply. His mind was doused in a haze of pleasure. He couldn't take his eyes off the way she moved her lips back and forth along his cock.

Each stroke built the pressure inside him until he thought his balls would explode. His hands curled into tight fists and a low, long moan escaped him when her left hand slid up his thigh to caress his ass.

Addie, I'm going to come if you do not stop, he panted.

Then, come, she responded, tightening her grip around his cock and sucking harder.

Merrick could feel his legs tremble as he fought against the powerful stimulation. A low cry built in his throat when she pulled back along his cock until only the bulbous head was in her mouth before she slid her lips back along his length, taking as much as she could without choking. The third time she did it, he couldn't hold back. The vision of her lips, taking him deep into her mouth, while sucking on him pulled him over the edge.

"Goddess!" He roared, shaking as he pulsed down her throat. "Addie...," he hissed, bowing his head and closing his eyes when another shudder ran through his frame.

He trembled as Addie slowly released her grip on his cock and ran a soothing caress over it with the tips of her fingers. His eyes slowly opened when he felt her hands running up his body again. The look in her gaze took his breath away. It was the same one that Borj's human had given to him.

His throat worked up and down as she cupped his face. Dropping his hands from the wall, he circled Addie's soft figure, drawing it against him and holding her close. Closing his eyes again, he just held her as he tried to understand what just happened.

It's called a blow job, Addie teased.

You will be doing that more often, he warned her. *It was incredible.*

Addie's sexy laugh stirred the desire inside him again. Her laughter died in a squeak of surprise when she felt his cock swell against her stomach. He captured her gasp in his mouth at the same time as he reached out and turned off the water that had begun to cool. He did not want anything to put out the fire that she had ignited.

"Merrick," Addie whispered when he pulled back and looked down at her.

"Now it is my turn, Addie," he warned her.

Addie nodded, not questioning that he was ready to go again. She was learning that he wasn't like a human male when it came to his physical needs. What he liked was that she didn't seem to care! Every time he touched her, he could sense her body's reaction to it and smell the tantalizing fragrance of her own arousal.

Opening the shower door, he stepped out and turned to help her out. He reached for the towel hanging from a long bar and tenderly dried her hair and back, before moving downward over her buttocks and legs. He took his time exploring her just like she had done to him. He worked his way back up when she turned so he could dry the front of her.

A mischievous grin curved his lips when he cupped the full mounds of her breasts. Leaning down, he sucked on each nipple until they were rosy and taut.

"I want you," she cried out, sliding her fingers into his wet hair and holding him against her breast.

"As you wish, my mate. Go lay on the bed, Addie," he replied, quickly drying his body. "I want you spread out for me."

A blush turned her cheeks a rosy color. He ran his fingers down one heated cheek before rubbing his thumb against her bottom lip. His eyes darkened when he saw the faint bruises on her neck and the thin pale line of where she had been shot.

"I am afraid of losing you," he said, surprising himself with his admission.

"You won't," she responded, rising up to brush a kiss across his lips. "I don't plan on going anywhere without you. Don't be too long."

Merrick nodded and watched as she turned and headed into the bedroom across the hall. His eyes swept down the curve of her back to her buttocks. Heat flooded him again. He would take her from behind this time. He wanted to bury himself as far as he could go inside her and cup her breasts as he fucked her.

He quickly finished drying his hair and body. Clutching the towel in one hand, he walked across the hallway to Addie's bedroom. She was laying on her back, her legs parted and her knees slightly bent. She had stacked the pillows up into a pile and was leaning against them. Her hands cupped her breasts and while her fingers played with her nipples.

"They tingled from your sucking," she said, starting to drop her hands back to her side.

"Don't, let me watch you play with them," he ordered, tossing the towel on the end of the bed. His eyes moved down to the thatch of blonde hair between her legs. "I want to see you pleasure yourself. Show me what feels good to you."

He watched Addie's eyes widen in surprise before she shyly nodded. His eyes followed her right hand as she slowly slid it down over her stomach to the silky strands covering her labia. Stepping forward, he kept his eyes glued to her fingers as she slid it between the soft folds. A low moan escaped her and her eyes drooped as she began rubbing tiny circles over the small nub.

Sinking down onto the end of the bed, he gently pushed her legs further apart. Her hips began rocking as she increased the speed. Soon, her left hand slid away from her breast to join her right one, parting the silky folds so she could have better access.

Merrick moved up the bed so he could take the place of her hands. Scooping her up, he settled behind her, spreading his legs on either side of hers. Sliding his hands down along her arms, he pressed them down to let her know that he wanted her to continue.

"Oh!" Addie whispered, leaning her head back against his shoulder.

Merrick slid his arms under hers and cupped her breasts in his hands. His eyes followed Addie's fingers and he mimicked the movement with his fingers on her taut nipples. He held her tighter when she began to move frantically, her breathing increasing as her orgasm built. Pinching her nipples, he watched as she jerked and shattered in his arms. Her loud cry drawing out until he felt as if he would join her.

Wrapping his arms around her, he rolled until she was lying face down on the bed. Scooting backwards, he gripped her hips and pulled her up onto her knees. His mind was a seething mass of hunger and all he could think about was her explosive orgasm and how her vaginal walls pulsed when she came.

He gritted his teeth and aligned his cock to her slick entrance. He was so sensitive that even the moist curls were almost painful. Leaning forward, he pushed into her heated channel until he was buried as deep as he could go.

For a moment he just held still, afraid that if he moved, he would come. Drawing in a deep breath, he tightened his fingers around her hips and began moving. The sight of his cock disappearing into her mesmerized him. He pulled back, panting as he did, before driving his hips forward so he could feel every delicious inch of her again and again. A low whimper escaped her each time he did it.

Merrick, that feels so good, she groaned.

How does this feel, Addie? He grounded out in a strained voice. *And, this.* Thrusting in and out again and again.

She answered him by spreading her knees a little further apart. Understanding what she wanted, his fingers bit into her flesh and he increased the speed of his thrusts until he could feel the heat exploding through her again. This time, her sweet ambrosia bathed his cock in its liquid essence. Pressing his hips against her ass, he felt his own release surge into her in wave after delicious wave.

Collapsing to the side, he cradled Addie against him. His arm wrapped tightly around her waist. Bending his head, he pressed a kiss against her damp shoulder.

I love you, Addie, he murmured. *Thank you for coming into my life.*

Anytime, she chuckled, sleepily. *Just so you know, I love you, too.*

I know. I read your thoughts, Merrick responded, teasing her.

I'll never be able to surprise you, she complained before releasing a big yawn and tucking her hand in his.

Sweet dreams, my mate, Merrick whispered, pressing another kiss to her shoulder.

He stared out the window of the bedroom waiting for his body to relax enough to pull out without waking her. From the light snores she was emitting, he doubted very much if anything would wake her. It had been a traumatic and busy day.

Restlessness moved through him. He didn't want to tell Addie, but he had sensed they were being watched back on the beach earlier. His natural warning system, heightened by living among the mountains, was never wrong.

Pulling away with regret, he rolled over and stood up. Taking care not to disturb her, he picked up a blanket lying on a nearby chair and covered her. He lightly stroked her hair before turning away.

Returning to the bathroom, Merrick quickly rinsed his body, dried, and dressed. He checked the weapons he had brought. Satisfied with what he had, he quietly checked the house to make sure it was secure before he exited through the rear door.

Moving silently down the back steps, he headed into the woods that surrounded the house. There was a light, northeasterly breeze blowing. It was time that the predators, who thought to hunt him again, became the prey.

Chapter 25

Addie sat up, disoriented for a moment before she twisted and pushed her hair out of her eyes. Something had woken her up. Turning again, her eyes swept the room for Merrick. He was gone. Glancing at the clock, she frowned when she saw that it was almost eleven.

Addie, someone is knocking on the door, Merrick said.

I'm coming, don't.... Her voice died when she realized that Merrick must have answered the door because she could 'hear' his side of the conversation with whoever was downstairs.

Scrambling out of the bed, she was jerking on her clothes. Grabbing her hairbrush out of the bathroom and a hair-band, she brushed it as she hurried down the stairs. An unfamiliar woman stood at the door, talking to Merrick as if she knew him.

Who is that? Addie asked with suspicion.

She says her name is Trudy Wilson, Merrick replied, turning to look at her. *She says she works for Cosmos Raines.*

Well, what does she want? Addie demanded, turning to glare at the woman.

"Hello, Addie," the woman said with a smile. "My name is Trudy Wilson. I work for Cosmos Raines Industries as part of his security team. I'm sorry to disturb you, but we have reason to believe that both you and Merrick are in danger."

"How did you know where I was?" Addie asked, coming to stand next to Merrick.

"It wasn't hard to figure out where you might go," Trudy responded, turning to look at Addie. "Unfortunately, we believe that those responsible for the attack on you this morning are also aware of it. A text message was sent to an unlisted number with this address."

"Who....?" Addie started to say before she remembered what Merrick had told her this morning. "Weston."

"Yes," Trudy replied with a nod. "RITA thinks that Weston Wright and Karl Markham are working together. If that is true, we need to get you both to a safe location as soon as possible."

Addie opened her mouth to ask Trudy where she suggested when Trudy's body jerked forward and her eyes widened in surprise. A small scream escaped Addie when Merrick suddenly wrapped his arm around her waist and took her to the floor. Trudy collapsed next to her, holding her side.

"Son-of-a-bitch," Trudy groaned. "Avery and Rose are going to toast my ass if I die."

"How bad is it?" Merrick asked, releasing Addie long enough to roll over to the wall so he could turn out the light.

"Hurts like hell, so that is a good sign, I guess," Trudy muttered. "I'd be more worried if I didn't feel anything."

"How bad?" Merrick demanded again, scooting across the floor so he could see for himself.

Trudy cried out when he rolled her onto her stomach and pulled her shirt up. Addie crawled over to see if she could help. Swallowing back the bile rising in her throat, she watched as Merrick tore a small section of Trudy's shirt and pressed it against the wound.

"The metal is still inside you," he said grimly.

"Thanks for that information, Doctor Alien," Trudy muttered sarcastically. "I think it is safe to say, we are in a shit load of trouble."

"Do you have a communication device on you?" Merrick asked.

"Yeah, left back pocket," Trudy moaned, lowering her head to the floor. "Right now would be a good time to call in some re-enforcements."

A deadly smile curved Merrick's lips. "I think that is an excellent idea," he said. "What is the code to get in?"

"Thumb print," Trudy mumbled, holding out her hand.

Addie watched as Merrick frowned down at the cell phone before glancing back at Trudy. Understanding what Trudy meant, she took the phone from Merrick and pressed Trudy's thumb to it. The moment it unlocked, she pressed the icon for the phone and punched in the number Merrick had given her before.

She held the phone out to Merrick when it showed it was connecting. Turning her attention back to Trudy, she laid her hand on the young woman's shoulder in comfort. Worry ate at her when she felt the woman's body begin to start shaking.

Merrick, I think she is going into shock, Addie sent to him.

Help will be here soon, he said.

Surprise widened Addie's eyes again when the sudden shimmer of light appeared. Glancing at Merrick, she saw the look of grim satisfaction on his face as several huge warriors stepped through the colorful doorway. Her lips formed a circle when she saw the figure of a slender woman slip through at the last minute before it close.

Addie recognized the woman from Reno. A large hole appeared in the wall next to where the door had been. The woman ducked, pulling a weapon from behind her back.

* * *

Merrick scowled at Core. A look of inquiry on his face. He had expected only his cousin, not the three other warriors and another human female.

"Who is she and what are Teriff, Derik, and Hendrik doing here?" He growled in a low voice.

"Teriff and Derik came to inform us that the council wants to meet with you tomorrow," Core snapped out. "Hendrik tagged along, and the female is Cosmos Raines' Head of Security and my bond mate."

"I am no one's mate," Avery snapped back. "Shit, Trudy. What the fuck are you doing here?"

Trudy turned her head with a moan. "Getting shot, what the hell does it look like?" She answered, before her head sank back to the floor. "It hurts. I knew it would, but damn, no one said it would hurt this bad."

"You two stay with Trudy," Merrick ordered. "There are at least two men. If possible, I want them both alive."

"Why?" Teriff demanded.

"They are the ones who held me captive. It is my right to seek Justice against them for the harm they have done," Merrick replied.

"Trudy needs medical attention," Avery said. "We have to get her out of here."

"I can open the Gateway for you," Core said with a relieved nod. "Derik, take the females back to Baade."

"I have a Portal device," Avery stated. "If he can carry Trudy, we'll get her to your medical unit."

Addie glanced frantically back and forth, trying to understand what they were saying. She ducked when another shot fired into the house. A hand threaded through her hair and she turned her head to see Merrick's glowing eyes staring fiercely at her.

"Go with them," he ordered.

Addie nodded, looking at him with wide, frightened eyes. *Where will you be?*

I am going to kill them, Merrick said, looking intently into her eyes. *I will not let them threaten or harm any others.*

Be careful, she whispered.

Addie watched as Merrick, and the other three men disappeared down the hallway toward the back family room. She jerked around when she felt a hand on her arm. The woman from Reno was motioning for her to follow as the younger male carefully lifted an unconscious Trudy into his arms.

The woman counted down from three before pressing the top of a silver cylinder. Addie's eyes widened as another shimmering doorway appeared. She could see movement on the other side. The woman rose and hurried through it, followed by the man carrying Trudy.

Addie rose to follow when a volley of bullets struck the walls around her. Crouching down, she glanced up in time to see the cylinder in the woman's hand, shatter as a bullet went through the doorway. As if by magic, the door disappeared.

Horror washed through Addie as she realized that she was alone. Turning on her hands and knees, she crawled further down the hallway until she was safe from any windows. Pressing her back against the wall, she glanced back and forth. The front room was out. Turning to look toward the back of the house, she decided to head for the family room.

Addie rolled onto her hands and knees and continued crawling. The moment she could, she struggled to her feet. One of the back windows was missing. She suspected that was how the men left the house. Unsure of what to do, she decided finding a place to hide was the best option. She and her siblings used to play hide and seek all the time and there were plenty of places throughout the house.

Glancing around, she tried to think of the best, and hardest to find, place to hide. Her eyes lit on the bookcase next to the fireplace. Her parents had remodeled the house years ago. The fireplace had a huge area behind it that was wasted space. Her dad had designed a false wall with built-in bookcase that was also a door to a storage closet.

Hurrying over to it, Addie pulled the candlestick latch and pulled it open. Stepping inside, she pulled the door closed behind her and turned on the light. The room was an odd shape, almost like a triangle, growing narrow and had a low ceiling toward the back and on one side. It was filled with beach and lake gear. She stepped around the chairs propped up against one wall and scooted the netted basket storage container on wheels out of the way.

Picking several beach blankets out of the basket, she piled them on the floor under the curved lower section of the staircase. Pulling a flashlight out of another basket, she turned it on and turned off the overhead light. Soon she was settled on the blankets in the corner. Afraid that even the dim light of her flashlight might somehow show where she was, she turned it off and settled down.

A shiver ran through her body. She didn't want to distract Merrick and fought the urge to reach out to him. Instead, she pulled one of the thick towels up around her shoulders and laid down. It didn't take long before her eyelids grew too heavy to hold up and her breathing settle down as she fell into a deep, exhausted sleep.

Chapter 26

Merrick moved silently through the darkness. He was in his realm when it came to tracking and hunting. Earlier today, he had scouted the area while Addie slept. The house was positioned between the ocean on one side and a small lake on the other. The closest house was at the beginning of the narrow road and was empty.

Teriff and Hendrik would take the back area around the lake, while he and Core would take the front that led to the ocean. They would make sweeps until they found the humans. Core paused, moving in a slow sweep about a hundred yards from the house.

He bent and picked up something off the ground. Merrick nodded when he saw the outline of the bullet casing. Pointing, he nodded for Core to go up into the tall trees. Within seconds, Core was moving swiftly upward.

Merrick paused again as the wind shifted. There was a faint scent to his right. Crouching, he moved slowly, making sure he stayed in the shadows. While there was a moon tonight, there were also clouds and a faint breeze. The combination made it more difficult to distinguish between natural and unnatural movement if a person knew how to use the shadows and the wind in their favor.

The Eastern Mountain Clan were renowned for their ghost-like movement through the forest. No one saw them unless they wanted to be seen. A whistle, too high to be heard by human hearing, sounded.

Core had seen something forty yards to the right. Merrick replied and changed course. There was a small patch of open ground between him and where he wanted to go. He could either go through it, or work his way around. Deciding it would be better to go around, he was about to turned and worked his way silently through the tall ferns when Core quietly called out.

The whistle warned him that there were three figures spread out. Merrick saw one of the figures rise up and throw something toward the house, before sinking back down into the tall ferns. Rage built up when a short time later, another figure rose up. This one had a long weapon, similar to what the men used during his captivity.

Focusing on the dark-clothed figure, he burst through the opening toward the male. He hit the male hard in the side, wrapping his arms around him and squeezing. He heard a loud roar and knew that Core had dropped down out of the trees and taken another male out.

Merrick knew immediately that something was wrong when the third person emitted a loud, terrified scream. Throwing the male in his arms away from him, he ignored the sickening thud and low cry of pain and fear.

"We didn't mean anything," the male he had thrown cried. "Please, it was just a joke! We were just joking."

Merrick released a low, menacing growl and crouched down in front of the crying boy. Core pulled the other two over and pushed them down on the ground in front of the tree. Merrick glanced at the weapon the one boy had been using.

Rising, he stepped over to it and picked it up. He looked at the metal and plastic toy before turning and walking back to squat down in front of the trio. Their being there was more than a joke.

"Who sent you?" Merrick demanded.

"Some... guy... He was at the gas station. He said he had a friend staying here and wanted to play a trick on him. All... All we were supposed to do is fire some paintballs at the house," the boy cried, holding his right leg. "He gave us a hundred bucks and told us there was another hundred after we got done."

Merrick lifted the paintball gun in his hand. With a quick twist, he broke it in two. Looking at the three boys, he snarled, feeling his teeth elongate in warning.

"Holy shit," one boy whispered. "We're gonna die."

"You will if you remain here," Core snapped in a quiet voice. "Run home."

The boys all nodded at the same time. Merrick stood and stepped back, glancing around the area. Something was wrong. Why would Weston and Markham use children? He glanced at the three boys. Two of them were helping the one he had thrown through the high ferns and onto the road.

"Addie," he whispered, turning to Core. "They wanted a distraction to get to Addie."

"She is safe," Core pointed out, looking back at the house.

"Yes, but they don't know that," Merrick replied, turning toward the house.

* * *

Addie jerked awake. Her hand slid to the wood floor beside her. She didn't know what had woken her, just a feeling that she wasn't alone any longer. Her heart raced with fear, but she forced herself to remain calm. Keeping her hand on the wood, she felt the slight vibration. Someone was inside.

Carefully twisting, she sat up and scooted further into the corner and waited. Her eyes flickered upward when she felt the slight brush of dust fall from above her head. Raising a trembling hand, she placed her palm against the underside of it.

She felt just the slightest vibration before it moved. Unfortunately, the dust that fell tickled her nose. Her hand flew to it just in time to muffle the sneeze that escaped her. Addie froze, glancing frantically upward wishing once again that she could hear. Raising her hand, she covered her nose and mouth to protect it from the dust.

Fear raced through her when she felt the shift in the wooden stairs above her head. This time, the movement appeared to be coming down. Closing her eyes, she reached instinctively for Merrick.

Merrick! Oh, God, please. Merrick!

Addie? Merrick's deep voice answered in surprise. *Where are you?*

In the house, she frantically thought back. *I think someone else is in here. I felt someone on the stairs, but I think they heard me sneeze. I can't hear them! Please, I'm scared.*

Where are you? He asked in an urgent voice.

There's a bookcase in the family room. Behind it is a storage closet. It is next to the fireplace, she responded. *Use the candlestick to open the door.*

I will come for you, he replied. *Do not move.*

I won't, she whispered, pulling her legs up and squeezing as far as possible into the corner. *Merrick...*

Yes, Addie.

I just want you to know that I love you, she said in a faint voice. *Please be careful.*

I love you, as well, my mate. I will be with you soon, he replied.

Addie leaned her head back, not wanting to know any longer where the bad guys were. Merrick was coming. That was all that mattered.

* * *

Merrick signaled to Core to find Teriff and Hendrik. Moving toward the house, he paused, looking up. One of the bedroom windows was open. Crossing around the back, he used the bannister and climbed up onto the roof over the wrap around porch. He stepped lightly up to the window and looked in. Fragments of broken glass lay on the carpet inside, while the twisted screen lay to the side of the window on the outside.

Stepping gingerly through the window, Merrick listened. The faint sound of footsteps below told him that the intruder was searching the house downstairs. He moved out of the bedroom and down the hallway. Stopping at the top of the stairs, he listened again. His head tilted when he heard the slight crunch of glass against the wood floor.

Whoever it was, they were in the foyer near the front of the house. The shot had shattered the small glass window in the front door, hitting Trudy. Turning the opposite way, he moved down the second set of stairs leading to the kitchen.

Merrick moved silently down the narrow staircase. It would be impossible to protect himself in the narrow space as there was no place to hide. He rounded the back of the kitchen which lead into the family room. His eyes scanned the area, stopping on the bookcase near the fireplace.

Addie, Merrick called.

Yes.

I am here, he replied in a gruff voice. *Stay hidden. I am on the other side of the bookcase.*

Be careful, she finally whispered.

I will. I promise.

Merrick slid back against the wall when he heard the sound of footsteps in the kitchen behind him. Reaching down to his waist, he pulled several small knives from his belt. Holding them in one hand, he slipped the first blade into the palm of his right hand. Waiting, he rounded the corner and tossed the blade.

The sickening sound of metal against flesh and the strangled cry of the male proved he had drawn first blood. A wild scattering of bullets swept the wall where Merrick had been standing only moments before. He had jumped over the long couch and ducked as the bullets ripped the plaster and sheetrock.

Rising up, he darted around the corner and back down the hallway. Turning the corner, he slipped up behind the kitchen from the other direction. A dark shape was bent over the center island. In the dim light, Merrick could see the blade sticking out of the man's shoulder.

Palming another blade, he cleared his throat. The man swiveled, off balance and raised the rifle in his hand. Merrick quickly threw three more blades. One hit the man he recognized as Weston in the left shoulder, the other embedded next to the one in his right shoulder and the third in his right thigh.

The rifle clattered to the floor of the kitchen just seconds before Weston slid down. He stared back at Merrick as he stepped into the room. Kicking the rifle to the side, Merrick knelt down in front of Weston.

"Where is Markham?" Merrick asked in a quiet voice.

"Fuck you," Weston replied.

Merrick reached out and twisted one of the blades in Weston's shoulder. Hoarse, agonizing screams pierced the air. Grabbing Weston by the neck, Merrick pushed his head back against the cabinet behind him.

"Where is Markham?" Merrick repeated.

"I... I... told you... to... fuck off," Weston bit out over the pain.

Merrick gripped the blade in Weston's thigh this time and turned it slowly. Weston's high pitched screams filled the air. Merrick turned slightly on his heel when a whistle warned him that Core had returned with Teriff and Hendrik. Pulling Weston up by the front of his shirt, he braced him against the cabinet.

"Are you going to kill him?" Core asked, looking at the pale features of the human and the blood pool under him.

"Not until I get the information I want from him," Merrick replied, glancing at Teriff. "I demand the Right of Justice."

"Granted," Teriff replied just as a neat hole appeared through the glass in the kitchen window and Weston's body jerked.

"Down," Merrick demanded, dropping Weston's body.

"That had to have been over two hundred yards away," Core cautioned. "I have been studying human weapons. There was no report so he must have a silencer on it."

Merrick's face turned grim as he studied Weston's lifeless body. This would not stop him from finding Markham. Turning his gaze to the other men, he looked at Teriff.

"That human is mine," he snarled.

"I do not think the human President of this country will complain if you take him out," Teriff replied. "If he does, I will send Borj and Tilly Bell to deal with him."

"I need to get Addie and take her from this place," he said, remaining low as he stepped into the other room.

"I thought she was already safe," Teriff replied, startled. "Did she not return with Derik?"

"No, and I wish to know why," Merrick retorted angrily.

He was carrying Trudy when the room was sprayed with gunfire, Addie explained. *Can I come out now?*

No, we will come in to you, Merrick said. *It is still too dangerous for you to come out.*

Weston?

Dead, but Markham is still out there, Merrick replied, pushing the candlestick down.

"Oh, Merrick," Addie murmured in a husky voice filled with relief when she saw him step through the opening.

Merrick opened his arms and wound them around her, resting his cheek against her hair. Briefly closing his eyes, he breathed in her familiar scent. Looking up, he nodded to Core who activated the Gateway.

I am going to take you to my home now, Merrick murmured, wrapping his arm around her waist.

* * *

Markham lowered the rifle in his hand. A brief sense of regret filled him before he pushed it away. Life was made up of life and death moments. As far as he was concerned, it had been Weston's time to die. Turning, he rose and moved away from the house.

His younger brother had gotten sloppy. He should have been in and out of the house in minutes. He had taken the shots, including the one that had hit the woman who had arrived unexpectedly, in an effort to warn his brother and give him time to escape.

A cold fury burned inside him as he strode back to his car which was parked at the deserted house at the entrance to the drive. He had realized immediately that things were not as they appeared. He had caught a brief glimpse of two men he didn't recognize heading toward the lake. They moved with a stealth and speed that reminded him of some of the big cats he had hunted.

He had quickly packed up, but he didn't have time to warn his brother. When he saw Weston's body hanging limply from the huge alien's grip, he knew that he couldn't chance his brother talking. He had taken the shot.

"I'll smoke an extra cigar for you Weston," Karl promised as he gently placed the case with his rifle in the back seat.

The only good thing that came out of the night was knowing that the alien male wasn't the only one. No, there were at least four of them. A smile curved his lips as he started the car and slowly pulled away from the house. He would need to reconsider how he was going to arrange his office, now that there were more specimens for display.

Chapter 27

Addie glanced around the long corridor that she was walking down the next morning. Merrick had apologized for having to leave so early, but he had a meeting to attend. She had risen when he did, smiling nervously at him when he brushed a kiss across her lips.

He hadn't said anything about having to remain in the room they had been shown to last night, so she figured it couldn't hurt to take a tiny look around. She was curious about what it would be like to be on another planet. Reaching up under the sleeve of the beautiful blue tunic she was wearing, she pinched her arm.

Nope, I'm not asleep, she thought as she looked over the sparkling white corridor with its curved arches and beautiful painted ceilings.

A startled squeak escaped her when she rounded a corner and ran into an older man just slightly taller than her. He was thin with shaggy brown hair and twinkling eyes. She watched as he straightened his glasses.

"So sorry about that," he said with an easy smile that faded as he studied her. "I don't believe I've met you."

A small scream escaped Addie when another figure appeared… out of the wall. The man turned and looked at the beautiful redhead as if it was normal for ghostly figures to just suddenly appear.

Addie took a step closer to the man when the figure walked toward her.

"Hi Addie, I'm RITA2," the redhead signed as she spoke. "I'm not a ghost. I'm an Artificial Intelligence program known as a Really Intelligent Technical Assistant. But, since Cosmos already had a RITA, I became RITA2, her twin. I've been working on creating a four-dimensional hologram that is not limited to the confines of..."

"Yes, thank you, that will be all RITA2," the man said in a distracted voice as he pushed his glasses further up on his nose. "You look just like Momma. By the way, I love your new glasses. They make you look more professional."

"Oh, thank you, Angus," RITA2 said. "I've scanned Addie. I need to look at some of the medical techniques. I'll be back later."

"Thank you again, RITA2," Angus Bell said with a sigh and a shake of his head. "I swear she might look like my mother, but she is my beautiful wife when it comes to personality."

"I heard that!" Tilly laughed in delight, coming up behind Angus and wrapping her arms around his waist before peeking at Addie. "Oh, more humans."

Addie shook her head. She had only gotten a fraction of what the ghostly creature had said, even though she had been using sign language. Addie had been too fascinated by the creature to understand everything she said. Gazing at the tiny woman and the disheveled man holding her, Addie decided that she had journeyed over the Rainbow to Oz.

"I'm Tilly Bell and this is my husband, Angus," Tilly introduced with a grin. "Welcome to Baade."

"I'm Addie," Addie replied, signing as she spoke.

"I know, Trudy was telling us all about you," Tilly said, wrapping her arm though Addie's.

"Trudy?" Addie murmured. "Is she alright?"

"Yes, you would like to go see her?" Tilly asked.

"I'm afraid that will not be possible," Merrick interjected, coming up and wrapping his arm around Addie's waist.

What is going on? Addie asked in confusion.

It would appear Trudy has been removed from the palace, Merrick answered.

Who… Never mind, Addie replied. *How was your meeting?*

It went well, Merrick replied before looking at Tilly and Angus, who were… kissing.

"If you will excuse us, I wish to speak with my mate," Merrick said politely.

"Are they always like that?" Addie asked, looking over her shoulder as Merrick guided her away.

"From what I have heard, yes," he responded quietly.

Addie frowned, glancing at Merrick's composed face. The constant ache of fear that had been with her the last few weeks returned. She didn't say anything, closing her mind in an effort to hide it from him as they made their way back to their rooms. She walked across the elegant living room, moving to the large set of windows overlooking a long garden.

Turning, she stared back at him and waited. He gazed at her for several long seconds before he walked over to her. Opening her mind, she tentatively reached for him.

* * *

Merrick knew the moment Addie opened her mind to him. He could feel her fear and worry. Striding over to her, he wrapped his hands in her silky hair and captured her lips in a kiss that left her dazed and breathless.

"You have nothing to fear, Addie," Merrick said in a husky voice.

"Something has happened," she whispered.

Merrick sighed and slowly nodded his head. "Yes."

"Did the council... Did they say that I couldn't stay?" She asked in a small voice, looking at his chest.

No! No, the council is very happy that I have found you. In fact, the success of finding so many bond mates has made them more receptive to letting warriors search for more, he said, tilting her head back. "But, my experience has also proven that there is a great need for caution as well."

"So, what are you not telling me?" She asked when he looked away.

"They have asked me to forgo my request for Right of Justice against Markham and join them on the council," Merrick said in a hard voice. "They want me to leave him to the human government. It was decided tracking him down would jeopardize further missions to Earth."

"I can understand that. Now that the government is aware of Markham, surely they will find and stop him," Addie responded, noting that he continued to avoid looking her in the eye.

"I do not trust that the human government will do anything about him," Merrick admitted.

"There's something else bothering you, isn't there? It isn't just Markham?" Addie asked.

"No, the position would also mean frequent travel between our home in the Eastern Mountains and the palace," Merrick explained.

"And…?" Addie asked, looking at Merrick with a puzzled look. "What are you really not telling me?"

"He is trying to avoid telling you there might be a procedure that can restore your hearing," RITA2 signed, suddenly appearing next to them.

Merrick's arms tightened around Addie when she emitted a loud squeak at RITA2's sudden presence. Frustration and fear rolled through him at the thought of hurting Addie in any way, and that included giving her a false sense of hope. The procedure wasn't proven because there had never been a case such as Addie's. When RITA2 had approached him about it earlier, he had dismissed her. She had appeared as he was leaving the Council chambers and said that her initial scans showed that the procedure had an eighty-two percent chance of success.

"I told you I would tell her," Merrick growled with a dark frown.

"Restore my hearing…" Addie whispered, raising a hand to touch her left ear. Hope blossomed in her. Was it really possible for her to actually hear again? "Merrick?"

"There is a slight chance that it would not be successful," Merrick replied.

"But, there is an even bigger chance it might," Addie exclaimed as excitement built inside her. "If I could hear again, even just a little… I would be able to hear your voice."

"I like talking to you in your head," he muttered, glaring at RITA2, who was looking at her fingernails. "You are a menace. You were the one who discouraged the council from allowing me the Right of Justice against Markham."

"Yes, having Prime warriors running around Earth looking for females will be bad enough, having them running around killing bad men would be too alien invasion. That creates a dreadful Public Relations nightmare. The humans would simply have a meltdown. Besides, you will love me once Addie can hear again," RITA2 laughed. "Oh, and just so you know, I'm working with RITA to find Markham for Avery. She'll catch him. Now, I need to do a few more tests to make sure the procedure will work for you Addie. Merrick is right. There's a slight chance that the surgery won't work… but, it's a small percentage based on my scans and calculations."

Merrick watched as Addie touched her ear and bit her lip. When she looked up at him with a gaze filled with hope, he knew he would support her in anything she wanted to do. Nodding, he smiled and brushed another kiss to her lips before pulling back and resting his forehead against hers.

No matter what, I love you the way you are, he whispered.

I love you, too, Addie smiled, before throwing her arms around his neck and hugging him close. *And I swear, I'll never complain about you thinking too much again.*

Good, because I have some really great thoughts going on in my head right now, he whispered, before he glanced over his shoulder. "You've won, now get out. I'll bring her to medical later for your testing. But, right now, she is all mine."

RITA2's eyes rolled as she turned on her delicate heels and headed for the door. "I swear Tilly and Angus are contagious. Every warrior that comes into the palace ends up with a one track mind!"

"I can think of worse things, my dear," a deep male voice replied right before the figure of a huge warrior materialized.

"DAR?" RITA2 whispered. "You've got your programming finished."

"With a little help from Tilly and Cosmos," DAR replied as he wrapped an arm around RITA2's slender waist. "Would you like to see some of it?"

RITA2's delicate eyebrow rose and a mischievous smile curved her lips. "You bet your server I do," she growled. "Make it late, Merrick. I might need more time."

Merrick and Addie watched in a combination of astonishment and amazement as the two figures dissolved. Merrick turned to look back down at Addie's glowing face. Late afternoon would work for him as well.

Epilogue

Two months later:

Merrick stood looking out the window. He had been traveling back and forth to Earth over the past two months. He had made a promise to Addie and he had kept it. It had taken that amount of time to get everything approved and set up for her parents to come to Baade. Today was the big day. Addie would be coming out of surgery in the few minutes.

He glanced at the older couple sitting at the table in the corner. They had agreed that for now, they would be the only ones to know about him and Addie. His thoughts flew back to the day two months ago when he and Addie had slipped through the Gateway into the living room of Robert and Helen Banks' home. It had helped that Avery had agreed to be there before they arrived to apprise them of what to expect.

Both of them had still been stunned when they walked through the Gateway. Well, stunned might be a little mild. Shaken, certainly, shocked, undoubtedly, terrified… positively. But, they had listened to them. He remembered talking to Robert alone later that evening while Addie, Avery, and Helen sat outside on the deck.

"Is she safe on your world?" Robert had asked, nervously twisting the glass of whiskey he held between his hands.

"Yes," Merrick replied. "I would protect Addie with my life."

"You know about her... hearing loss," Robert continued with a deep sigh. "Helen has always felt guilty about Addie losing her hearing. She hadn't realized just how sick Addie was. She thought it was just a bad cold."

"Addie does not blame anyone for her hearing loss," Merrick replied in a low voice. "I want you to know that there is a chance that Addie's hearing can be restored. Our medical technology is more advanced than yours, but there is still a chance that it will not work."

"What does Addie say?" Robert asked.

"She is excited," Merrick said, deciding it was probably best not to tell the man that he could talk to his daughter without the need to say anything out loud. "I would like for you and your mate to be there when Addie has the procedure done. I know she misses you, but she wanted to prove that she could be independent."

"We miss her, too," Helen's soft voice had said from the doorway of the kitchen. "I'm afraid I became overprotective after... after her illness. I would like to be there when she has the surgery, if you are sure she won't be upset."

Merrick shook his head. "She would be honored to have you there, just as I would," he said, rising out of his seat. "We would like to visit again, if you don't mind. I think Addie would enjoy it."

The first visit had gone better than either one of them had expected. Helen had finally broken down and talked to Addie about her feelings of guilt at not taking her to the doctor sooner. Addie admitted that while being deaf was difficult, she had also learned a great deal about herself and discovered that she was much stronger than she realized.

After several visits, Addie decided to tell her parents about the surgery. She had been afraid if it didn't work, they would be disappointed and feel guilty again. It had taken some gentle persuasion from Merrick to convince her that they would support her either way.

"I hope the surgery works," she said late one night after they returned from another brief visit. "I told my mom about it tonight. She wants to be here."

"If you wish for them to be here, I will make sure they are," he promised. "They love you very much. They will support you whatever happens."

She had sighed again before nodding. "You're right," she agreed. "I love you, Merrick. Thank you for supporting me."

Merrick bowed his head, remembering how nervous she had been when the healer took her back for the surgery two hours earlier. He turned when the door opened. The healer, followed by RITA2, stepped into the room. The pleased smiles on their faces was encouraging.

"She is in recovery," the healer said. "The surgery went well. The crystal regeneration and rebuilding of the hair cells needed for hearing were successful. I must caution though, her left ear was in worse condition so she may still have a minor hearing loss in that ear."

"When can we see her?" Merrick asked.

"You can go in now," the healer said. "We sedated her so that she would not move during the surgery, more for her own comfort than a necessity."

Merrick nodded, standing to the side as Robert and Helen asked numerous questions. He didn't care about any except the fact that Addie would be awake soon. At least, he didn't think he cared about anything until he heard RITA2 congratulating Helen and Robert.

"Congratulations?" Merrick repeated. "Congratulations for what?"

RITA2's laughter filled the area. "You are going to be the father of twin girls," RITA2 replied. "Prime males are extremely potent. There is a chemical in their bites that is released during mating that has a huge effect on human females causing them to have twins. Not only that, just about all the babies born are female. The Prime males love it!"

"Twins…," Merrick said, swaying as what RITA2 was saying sunk in. "Does… Does Addie know?"

"Not yet," RITA2 said mischievously before she began to fade. "The scans indicate she is almost a month along."

Merrick nodded, a grin lighting his face as he remembered her complaining just this morning of being sick at her stomach. They both thought it was because of her being nervous about the surgery. Now, he realized the nausea might have been caused by an entirely different reason.

He followed behind the healer, Robert, and Helen as they walked down the corridor in the medical unit. Turning the corner, he recognized the room they were entering as the one he had occupied a few short months ago. He stood behind them as Addie turned her head to look at her parents.

"Addie," Helen said, smiling hopefully as she stepped into the room.

"What...?" Addie whispered, shock flickering across her face as she stared back and forth between her parents, the healer, and Merrick. "Mom," Addie said hoarsely, raising her hand up to her. "Mom, it's okay...."

"Oh, Addie," Helen said in a voice thick with tears. "I thought... I hoped... It doesn't matter. All that matters is that you are happy and that you and the...."

"Helen, let Merrick sit with Addie," Robert interrupted, pulling her away from the side of the bed.

"Oh, Robert," Helen whispered. "I really hoped it would work."

Merrick stepped around the healer, Robert and Helen and sank down on the bed next to Addie. Brushing her hair back from her forehead, disappointment for her fought with the overwhelming happiness. It wasn't a very difficult battle. His joy over her expecting their babies was too much to be shadowed.

I love you, Addie, Merrick said in a voice filled with tenderness. *It doesn't matter. All that matters is that we are together with the babies.*

Babies?! What babies? Addie asked in confusion.

Ours, Merrick replied, lifting her hand to his lips. *RITA2 says that you are almost a month along with twin girls. We are going to be parents.*

He watched as Addie's face softened with love and amazement. Gripping his fingers, she pulled his hand down over her stomach. A mischievous grin lit her eyes.

"I love you," Addie whispered, staring up into his eyes. "Mom, Dad..."

"Yes, sweetheart," Helen said, turning to look back as Merrick helped her to sit up.

"I can hear you," Addie whispered, her eyes glowing as she stared up at Merrick. "Have I told you how much I love the sound of all of your voices?"

Shock and joy flashed across Merrick's face as he pulled her into his arms. Addie buried her face in his neck, uncaring that she was crying. She could hear the laughter and choked sobs coming from her and her mother. But the greatest thing was she could hear Merrick's rich, smooth voice telling her over and over how much he loved her.

"I love you, Merrick," she sniffed, wiping at her tears as she looked up at him.

"I love you more, Addie," Merrick said, brushing a kiss across her damp cheeks. *But, I still plan on thinking too much.*

A rosy blush swept across her cheeks as some of the things he was thinking formed in her mind. The healer, seeing Merrick's glance, chuckled as he ushered Helen and Robert out of the room and instructed RITA2 to lock the door. Some things were best said in private.

To Be continued.... **Core's Attack**

Characters' Relationships:

Teriff, Prime Leader of Baade - **mated to** Tresa: four sons, J'kar, Borj, Mak, and Derik and one daughter, Terra

Angus and Tilly Bell, humans – married: three daughters, Hannah, Tansy and Tink

Warriors of Baade:

J'kar 'Tag Krell Manok **mated to** Jasmine 'Tinker' Bell: twin daughters, Wendy and Tessa

Borj 'Tag Krell Manok **mated to** Hannah Bell: twin boy & girl, Sky and Ocean

Mak 'Tag Krell Manok **mated to** Tansy Bell: twin daughters, Sonya and Mackenzie

Terra 'Tag Krell Manok **mated to** Cosmos Raines

Derik 'Tag Krell Manok **mated to** Amelia Thomas aka Runt

Members of Cosmos' security team:

Garrett	Avery
Trudy	Rose
Rico	Maria

Prime Warriors of Bade:

Merrick, Eastern Clan Leader, **mated to** Addie Banks

Core **mated to** Avery

Lan **mated to** Natasha

Brock **mated to** Helene

Lal **mated to** Ava Raines

Gant, Western Plains Clan Leader

Brawn, Desert Clan Leader
Bullet, Southern Clan Leader, **mated to** Maria
Hendrik, Northern Clan Leader – Trudy Wilson

RITA (Earth) **zapped by** FRED
RITA2 (Baade) **zapped by** DAR

If you loved this story by me (S.E. Smith) please leave a review. You can also take a look at additional books and sign up for my newsletter at **http://sesmithfl.com** to hear about my latest releases or keep in touch using the following links:

Website: http://sesmithfl.com
Newsletter: http://sesmithfl.com/?s=newsletter
Facebook: https://www.facebook.com/se.smith.5
Twitter: https://twitter.com/sesmithfl
Pinterest: http://www.pinterest.com/sesmithfl/
Blog: http://sesmithfl.com/blog/
Forum: http://www.sesmithromance.com/forum/

Excerpts of S.E. Smith Books

If you would like to read more S.E. Smith stories, she recommends Hunter's Claim, the first in her Alliance series. Or if you prefer a Paranormal or Western with a twist, you can check out Lily's Cowboys or Indiana Wild...

Additional Books by S.E. Smith

Short Stories and Novellas

For the Love of Tia
(Dragon Lords of Valdier Book 4.1)
A Dragonling's Easter
(Dragonlings of Valdier Book 1.1)
A Dragonling's Haunted Halloween
(Dragonlings of Valdier Book 1.2)
A Dragonling's Magical Christmas
(Dragonlings of Valdier Book 1.3)
A Warrior's Heart
(Marastin Dow Warriors Book 1.1)
Rescuing Mattie
(Lords of Kassis: Book 3.1)

Science Fiction/Paranormal Novels

Cosmos' Gateway Series

Tink's Neverland (Cosmos' Gateway: Book 1)
Hannah's Warrior (Cosmos' Gateway: Book 2)
Tansy's Titan (Cosmos' Gateway: Book 3)
Cosmos' Promise (Cosmos' Gateway: Book 4)
Merrick's Maiden (Cosmos' Gateway Book 5)

Curizan Warrior

Ha'ven's Song (Curizan Warrior: Book 1)

Dragon Lords of Valdier

Abducting Abby (Dragon Lords of Valdier: Book 1)
Capturing Cara (Dragon Lords of Valdier: Book 2)
Tracking Trisha (Dragon Lords of Valdier: Book 3)
Ambushing Ariel (Dragon Lords of Valdier: Book 4)
Cornering Carmen (Dragon Lords of Valdier: Book 5)
Paul's Pursuit (Dragon Lords of Valdier: Book 6)
Twin Dragons (Dragon Lords of Valdier: Book 7)

Lords of Kassis Series

River's Run (Lords of Kassis: Book 1)
Star's Storm (Lords of Kassis: Book 2)
Jo's Journey (Lords of Kassis: Book 3)
Ristéard's Unwilling Empress (Lords of Kassis: Book 4)
Magic, New Mexico Series
Touch of Frost (Magic, New Mexico Book 1)
Taking on Tory (Magic, New Mexico Book 2)
Sarafin Warriors
Choosing Riley (Sarafin Warriors: Book 1)
Viper's Defiant Mate (Sarafin Warriors Book 2)
The Alliance Series
Hunter's Claim (The Alliance: Book 1)
Razor's Traitorous Heart (The Alliance: Book 2)
Dagger's Hope (The Alliance: Book 3)
Zion Warriors Series
Gracie's Touch (Zion Warriors: Book 1)
Krac's Firebrand (Zion Warriors: Book 2)
Paranormal and Time Travel Novels
Spirit Pass Series
Indiana Wild (Spirit Pass: Book 1)
Spirit Warrior (Spirit Pass Book 2)
Second Chance Series
Lily's Cowboys (Second Chance: Book 1)
Touching Rune (Second Chance: Book 2)
Young Adult Novels
Breaking Free Series
Voyage of the Defiance (Breaking Free: Book 1)

Recommended Reading Order Lists:

http://sesmithfl.com/reading-list-by-events/
http://sesmithfl.com/reading-list-by-series/

About S.E. Smith

S.E. Smith is a *New York Times*, *USA TODAY*, *International, and Award-Winning* Bestselling author of science fiction, fantasy, paranormal, and contemporary works for adults, young adults, and children. She enjoys writing a wide variety of genres that pull her readers into worlds that take them away.

CPSIA information can be obtained
at www.ICGtesting.com
Printed in the USA
BVHW04s1000280818
525722BV00050B/378/P